THE HUDDERSFIELD JOB

Out in the windswept fastness of North Yorkshire's Fylingdales Moor stands the impregnable fortress which houses the complex radar equipment that is a vital part of the West's early warning system against attack by intercontinental ballistic missiles. It also houses a traitor because the system, designed never to break down, mysteriously does. Marcus Farrow, ex-newspaper man and one-time naval commando, together with his colleagues Jock Harris and Charlie McGowan, move in swiftly to find out why, how and by whom the sabotage was effected.

THE HUDDERSFIELD JOB

Angus Ross

A Lythway Book

CHIVERS PRESS
BATH

First published 1971
by
John Long Limited
This Large Print edition published by
Chivers Press
by arrangement with
the author
1992

ISBN 0 7451 1541 1

British Library Cataloguing in Publication Data available

This one is for
my daughter Anne

SATURDAY

They came to get me at half past two in the morning. Jock Harris, and a man I had never seen before. Jock banged on the door of my new—courtesy of H.M. Government—caravan, and didn't leave off until I'd rolled out of my bunk and opened up. It was cold, but fine. There was a lot of starlight and a full, pale moon. I stood on the step looking down at him, still half asleep.

'Jock? What's up?'

'Get dressed,' he said.

He followed me inside and sat on the other bunk while I splashed cold water over my face and dragged some clothes on. As I leaned across his shoulder to plug in my razor, he shook his head.

'You'll do as you are. Just get your coat. We're in a hurry.'

His manner said no questions, and I shrugged into my raincoat. Then, as we were set to go, I unlocked the metal drawer set into the woodwork under my bunk and took out the Smith & Wesson. I held the gun in its little home-made holster flat on the palm of my hand, let him see it. He hesitated, then nodded.

'I don't think so, but you never know. Bring it anyway. Come on, let's get moving.'

As I locked the caravan, I heard a car start. The eager shape of a Rover 3500 moved up from behind the hedge and, when Jock opened the door, I caught a glimpse of the driver in the faint green glow from the instrument panel. A man of about thirty-five, bulky in his Crombie overcoat, with receding hair and rimless spectacles. I ducked into the back, and Jock sat up front with his right arm along the top of the driving seat. He looked at me over his shoulder.

'This is Charlie McGowan. Charlie—Mark Farrow.'

Charlie dropped into drive and looked up as we moved off to give me a short nod in the rear-view mirror. That was it. For all I knew he might have been dumb. But he could drive, all right. He handled the doctored car like a professional. We turned south at the lane's end and he gunned the motor up through the gears. Mercifully, the winding road was dry and quite deserted. A moon-bathed Holmes Chapel flitted eerily by like a silent film run much too fast, and we hit the M6 doing well over the ton. With the engine noise settled down to a steady muted roar, Jock half turned.

'We're going down to see the Man,' he said. 'Don't ask us why. You know as much as we do.'

'In that case,' I turned sideways and hunched down in the corner, 'you won't mind if I resume my hard-earned kip.'

2

As I was settling down, I caught Charlie quizzing me again in the mirror. His expressionless look gave me a curious tight sensation in the chest and I remember feeling glad, even then, that he was on our side. I do not sleep easy in cars being driven very fast by people I don't know, but with Charlie I never gave it a thought. Next thing I knew, Jock was leaning over the squab to prod me in the ribs, and I was yawning at the lions in a deserted Trafalgar Square.

Charlie swung the Rover in under a narrow arch, and parked neatly alongside the only other car on the rectangle. One which made ours look like a kiddy's plaything. We got out, me stiffly, and headed across the yard for the back door. Charlie showed his buzzer to the big Marine sergeant who barred our way, and another boot-neck preceded us down the barracks-like corridor. In the lift, I looked at my watch. Then I looked at it again. But I'd seen it right the first time. It still said only twenty past five.

Miss Hetherington was waiting at the tall double doors, and I thought for one foolish moment she was going to break down and admit to knowing us. She looked exactly as I remembered her. Same twin set, same tweed skirt, same sensible shoes. She pushed one side of the doors wide open, and stood back to let us enter.

'Please go in. He will be with you in a

3

moment.'

We filed inside in what I supposed was the correct order of seniority. Charlie first, then Jock, and me a long way last. I felt the same clutching of the carpet at my unworthy feet, and my eyes went to the vast and beautiful Turner on the wall behind the desk. The room was definitely smaller than the main hall in the Gallery across the way, and the high walls were not quite so cluttered, but they still carried a lot of canvas. About as much as a three-masted barque. There were enough *objets* in the place, even excluding the furniture, to give Sotheby's a small fortune in commission alone. We were all standing there, just looking at it, when he came in at the other door and walked smiling towards us.

I actually felt myself blink. So much for those weeks of training at the big house in Sutherland. But I'd been all set for the black coat and striped trousers bit. Instead, he was wearing a beautiful soft tweed, heavy silk shirt of palest gold, and dull bronze tie. Then I realised what day it was, and that this had to be his going-home-for-the-weekend gear. His shoes, which had the shine and texture of a newly opened chestnut, must have cost more than my entire rig-out. I tried to remember whether, in the morning's rush, I'd put on clean underwear. He moved in behind his big desk, and waved us to chairs. Miss

4

Hetherington came in by the same door, and put two files in front of him. He gave the old doll a smile, then looked at each of us in turn.

'Tea, gentlemen?' Without waiting for us to reply, he nodded. 'Yes, tea, Miss Hetherington. And toast. Rather a lot of toast, eh?'

She left without uttering a word. Come to think of it, none of us had uttered a word. In the presence of the Man, they come not all that easy. He always seemed to say enough for everybody. He started now without preamble, his hands busy with the seal on the first of the files.

'Now, gentlemen. What do you know about Fylingdales?' We opened our mouths to tell him, but he wasn't having any. 'Fylingdales,' he went on, 'is what used to be a damn good grouse moor. It's in Yorkshire, about eight miles south of Whitby. It is the location of one of the three ballistic missiles early-warning stations which protect the Western powers against surprise attack. The other two are at Thule in Greenland and at Clark in Alaska. These three stations comprise a radar system which, since its completion in 1962, has been a constant and most effective shield against any nonsense from the Others.'

We waited. So far, he'd told us nothing we didn't already know. But we knew too that he hadn't got us out of bed in the middle of the night just to preach a lesson in basics. Miss

Hetherington came in carrying more, probably, on her big silver tray than she'd ever attempted before. Being nearest, I jumped up to help her. It was a mistake. She didn't say anything, but I sensed by the imperceptible pursing of her thin lips that I was out of order. So I sat down and watched her hump her burden over to the corner of his desk. She gave to each of us an immaculate linen napkin, an exquisite plate, and pale top-people's tea in a cup out of which I was frightened to drink. She had conjured up what looked at first glance like a great deal of toast, but it was all cut into tiny squares and I could have eaten the lot myself. She sneered invisibly at our various juggling acts, then silently withdrew.

As we nibbled, the Man told us something we *didn't* already know.

'Gentlemen,' he shot a cuff to look at his watch, 'this morning, at one o'clock precisely, there was a malfunction at Fylingdales which put the whole shooting match out of action for a little over eight minutes.'

He paused, waiting for one of us to comment. We all looked at Charlie. He leaned forward to put his cup and saucer on the little mat placed near the edge of the big desk by the diligent Miss Hetherington, and cleared his throat.

'That sounds, sir, like a pretty quick repair job.'

'Quite,' the Man agreed drily, 'except that

the equipment at Fylingdales—which, incidentally, is far and away the most sophisticated of its kind in the world—is designed never to *need* any repair. It is further designed, should the impossible manage perversely to happen, to repair itself automatically by switching immediately to one of two parallel systems which stand permanently ready.'

'Sabotage.'

Soon as I'd said it, I felt a damned fool. Their three pairs of eyes feasted on my hot face. But the Man just nodded.

'Of course,' he said soberly. 'Dirty work at Fylingdales. And at Thule in Greenland ... *and* at Clark in Alaska. All synchronised to the split second. Most perturbing. It was all we could do to dissuade our friends across the sea from pressing their little buttons.'

Charlie had been polishing his rimless specs. He put them back on. 'Sir,' he said, 'do we know anything at all?'

The Man sat back in his chair. 'Oh yes, we've a jolly good idea how it was done. But of course the mechanics of the thing are not important. What we want to know, and very damn quick about it, is *why* it was done and *by whom*.'

Then Jock made his little contribution. He gestured towards the files lying on the Man's broad desk. 'Anything to go on, sir?'

'Yes, there is.' The Man nudged the files

7

with the point of the ancient poniard he used as a paper-knife. 'Here are two sets of files, one lot full and one abbreviated, of five different people on the Fylingdales technical staff. No need to clutter you chaps with the details, but we're sure that one or more of them must have engineered this thing. As I've said, we want very rapidly to know who it was and why he, or they, did it.'

He looked at us, and we looked at one another. 'More tea, gentlemen? No? Then I'll let you get on ... ' He rose, and we all stood up. He turned at the door and nodded at Charlie. 'Take care of the files, McGowan. I shall look forward to hearing from you.'

Then he was gone, and Jock was at the teapot. Miss Hetherington came in as he was topping us all up, and frowned. When Jock returned the big silver pot to its stand she picked up the tray, racks of toast and all, and took it away. Jock grinned.

'Bloody miserable old bitch. What *she* needs is a good stiff...'

I heard her coming back, and flashed him a warning frown. She was holding a sheaf of travel warrants, and addressed herself to Charlie.

'We have reserved two compartments on the 0800 from King's Cross to York Central. You're to leave the car in the station forecourt. It will be collected. Here are the keys to another vehicle with the same registration number. You will find it in the drive at the side of the Station Hotel in York. He says you're to report any development most urgent.'

She looked around for our cups. I'd hidden mine in the pile of the carpet. I was hoping Miss Hetherington might stick her foot in it. If not, the Man could use it for practising his putting shots. We trooped out, Charlie with his files and his travel warrants. I thought there would be a production about taking them out of the building, but Miss Hetherington must have passed the word. All we got from the bloke on the door was a respectful salute. Outside, the big black car was gone. We eased into the Rover, and Charlie drove us up to King's Cross.

We were early, so sat in the car until just before train time. I wondered why *two* compartments, but hadn't liked to ask. Now I got it. Our own first-class compartment was right at the end of a coach. The one next to it was empty, and locked. Anybody wanted to look or listen, he'd have to clamber outside on the roof. We let ourselves in. Jock dropped into a corner seat with a thankful sigh.

'Jesus,' he said, 'what a relief. All I need now is a bloody good breakfast.'

Charlie looked at him. 'Right, then,' he said tonelessly. 'They should start serving it soon as we pull out. You go first.'

Give old Jock his due, he didn't linger. While

9

he was gone, Charlie and I set about reading the files. When Jock returned from the dining car, Charlie gave me the nod. I ate as quickly as I comfortably could. By this time the train was really moving. I lurched back to our compartment just as Charlie was finishing his current file. He got up, and went off without a word.

'Christ,' I said, 'is he always like this?'

'Yes,' Jock said. 'Always. You'll need to get used to him. Tell you what though'—he paused to suck hard at something caught in one of his back teeth—'I'm damned glad old Charlie is with us on this one. So might you be, laddie, before we've got it sorted out.'

He went back to his reading, and I to mine. The comprehensive files were something to see, and I felt a pang of disquiet in the knowledge that C.I.H. must have at least this much dope on me. Charlie returned and, as the train rocketed along the continuous welded line, we passed the files from hand to hand and read in silence. Later, we quizzed each other on the content of the short ones. Charlie kept us at it until we stopped making mistakes.

Subject: BARRY ALAN KEMP
Nationality: British. Date of birth 3:5:1939 at 4, The Drive, Hendon, London NW4. Present address: 51, Carter Lane, Pickering, Yorks. Wife: Ruth, *née* Goldman; born Hendon,

London 12:8:41. Children: son Benjamin, born Pickering, Yorks., 19:7:69.

DESCRIPTION: Height: five feet eight inches. Weight: 144 lb. Complexion: dark. Hair: black, worn medium, full beard. Eyes: black. Build: slight. Spec. peculiarities: left eye artificial (fireworks accident 1947); sardonic wit, tends to gesticulate. Skills: expert on computers and radar, excellent bridge player. Religion: Jewish. Education: St. Paul's School, Finchley, London 1944–9: Bishop Amsden Prep. School, Finchley, London 1949–57; Cambridge University (King's—B.Sc., Ph.D.), 1957–62. Professional: Radio Corp. of America radar school at Henley-on-Thames 1962; joined Fylingdales 1963. Politics: Conservative. Hobbies: bridge, music, the theatre; non-drinker.

PARENTS: Michael Alan Kemp (*né* Karminski—name changed by deed poll, London 1936) antique dealer (silver), born Stepney, London, 1913. Died ... Ruth, *née* Silberman, housewife, born Stepney, London 1915. Died...

GRANDPARENTS (paternal): Benjamin Karminski, silversmith, born Omsk, Russia, 1872. Emig. to Glasgow 1912. Moved to London 1913. Died Stepney, London 1944. Nadja, *née* Desnovitch, housewife, born Omsk,

Russia 1878. Emig. to Glasgow 1912. Died Hendon, London, 1956.

GRANDPARENTS (maternal): Jack Silberman, butcher, born Stepney, London 1883. Died Stepney, London 1961. Janet, *née* Samuels, housewife, born Stepney, London 1885. Died Stepney, London 1969.

SIBLINGS: sister, Janet Kemp, physiotherapist, born Hendon, London 27:4:42. Died...
Ends.

Subject: HAROLD SUTCLIFFE
Nationality: British. Date of birth: 20:3:47 at 3, Warner's Fold, Moortop, Barnsley, Yorks. Present address: 7, Bishop St., Robin Hood's Bay, Yorks. Wife—(bachelor). Children: none known.

DESCRIPTION: Height: five feet ten inches. Weight: 190 lb. Complexion: swarthy. Hair: dark, worn short; clean-shaven. Eyes: grey. Build: strong, thickset. Spec. peculiarities: nose broken and re-set, thickening of left ear, scar on back of left hand. Skills: good rugby (League) player, radar expert. Religion: Methodist (occasional). Education: Barnsley Moortop Jnr. school 1952–8; Barnsley Technical College 1958–64; Leeds University (B.Sc.) 1965–9. Professional: Radio Corp. of America radar school at Henley-on-Thames Sept.–Dec. 1969; joined Fylingdales Jan. 1970. Politics: Labour. Hobbies: rugby; sea-fishing; moderate (beer) drinker.

PARENTS: Herbert Sutcliffe, miner, born Barnsley, Yorks., 1920. Died (mine accident) 1963. Rita, *née* Fowler, school-meals worker, born Barnsley 1923. Died...

GRANDPARENTS (paternal): Harold Everett Sutcliffe, miner, born Barnsley, Yorks., 1898. Died Barnsley, Yorks., 1967. Sarah, *née* Firth, housewife, born Barnsley, Yorks., 1902. Died...

GRANDPARENTS (maternal): Albert Firth, miner, born Barnsley, Yorks., 1901. Died Barnsley, Yorks., 1968. Blanche, *née* Spencer, housewife, born Ossett, Yorks., 1899. Died...

SIBLINGS: brother Albert Sutcliffe, miner, born Barnsley, Yorks., 17:5:1945. Died (mine accident) 1963; sister Mary Spencer Sutcliffe, schoolteacher, born Barnsley, Yorks., 1946. Died...
Ends.

Subject: STANLEY ELDON
Nationality: American. Date of birth: 27:8:41 at 1474a West 63rd Street, Newark, New Jersey,

U.S.A. Present address: 23 Hilltop Ave., Saddler's Rise, Whitby, Yorks. Wife— (bachelor). Children: none known.

DESCRIPTION: Height: five feet eleven inches. Weight: 180 lb. Complexion: fresh. Hair: fair, worn long; clean-shaven. Eyes: blue. Build: muscular, athletic. Spec. peculiarities: scar at left jawbone. Habits: takes nose between thumb and forefinger of right hand when annoyed or upset; an extrovert; effervescent. Skills: expert rally driver; good mechanic. Religion: Episcopalian. Education: Newark Jr. High School 1947–53; Newark College of Sciences 1953–8. Professional: U.S. Air Force, navigator, radar op., separated in Germany 1966; joined Radio Corp. of America (G.B.) Ltd. and trained at their radar school at Henley-on-Thames; started work Fylingdales 1967. Politics: Republican. Hobbies: motor cars, women; not known as a drinker.

PARENTS: Arthur Henry Eldon, regular soldier U.S. Army, born Newark, New Jersey, 1917. Died ... Hilda, *née* Peacock, housewife, born Oldham, Lancashire, England, 1921. Died...

GRANDPARENTS (paternal): Horace Stanley Eldon, textile worker, born Oldham, England 1893. Emig. U.S.A. 1912. Died Newark, New Jersey 1961. Anna, *née* Woscek, born Lodz,

Poland 1895. Emig. U.S.A. with parents 1901. Died Newark, New Jersey 1968.

GRANDPARENTS (maternal): Albert Peacock, textile worker, born Oldham, Lancashire 1895. Died Oldham, Lancashire 1963. Maude, *née* Edwards, housewife, born Royton, Lancashire 1900. Died...

SIBLINGS: brother Ernest Eldon, Lt. U.S. Air Force, born Oldham, Lancashire 1942. Died ... brother Horace Eldon, advertising agent, born Oldham, Lancashire 1945. Died ... sister Mary Eldon, stenographer, born Newark, New Jersey 1946. Died...
Ends.

Subject: JAMES ROBERT CHISHOLM
Nationality: British. Date of birth: 17:9:44 at 14, School Street, Huddersfield, Yorks. Present address: 23 Hilltop Ave., Saddler's Rise, Whitby, Yorks. Wife—(bachelor). Children: none known.

DESCRIPTION: Height: five feet seven inches. Weight: 180 lb. Complexion: ruddy. Hair: auburn, wavy, worn medium; clean-shaven. Eyes: brown. Build: very muscular, strong. Spec. peculiarities: cracks knuckles when ill-at-ease; scar across right eyebrow. Skills: expert computer man; crack shot with pistol;

fluent German. Religion: none (atheist). Education: Huddersfield West Junior School 1949–55; Huddersfield Grammar School 1955–62; Leeds University (B.Sc.) 1962–5 Professional: Ferranti Electronics, Manchester 1965–7; Radio Corp. of America school at Henley-on-Thames 1967; joined Fylingdales 1968. Politics: Labour, non-active. Hobbies: walking; shooting (pistol); reading. Introvert, non-gregarious. Drinks rarely.

PARENTS: Jesse Chisholm, textile worker, Petty Officer R.N. born Huddersfield, Yorks., 1917. Died (active service) 1944. Ilse, *née* Wager, born Lübeck, Germany 1923. (Sent to friends in Huddersfield 1939.) Died Innsbrück, Austria, 1964.

GRANDPARENTS (paternal): Robert Chisholm, textile worker, born Huddersfield, Yorkshire 1896. Died Barcelona, Spain 1939. Emily, *née* Robinson, housewife, born Huddersfield 1899. Died . . .

GRANDPARENTS (maternal): Gerhard Wager, leather merchant, born Bad Oldersloe, Schleswig-Holstein, Germany 1893. Died Buchenwald, Germany 1942. Anna, *née* Fischer, born Lübeck 1900. Died Buchenwald, Germany 1942.

SIBLINGS: none.
Ends.

Subject: JOHN WILLIAM (BILL) LAWSON
Nationality: British. Date of birth: 19:3:29, at
198 Leith Walk, Edinburgh. Present address:
Sea View, Moorside Road, Scarborough,
Yorks. Wife: Elizabeth Anne, *née* Scobie; born
Edinburgh 1931. Children: son Angus, born
Quendon, Essex 1962; daughter, Helen, born
Quendon, Essex, 1964; son, John Henry, born
Scarborough, Yorks., 1967.

DESCRIPTION: Height, six feet one inch. Weight:
214 lb. Complexion: fair. Hair: sandy,
thinning, worn short; clean shaven. Eyes: blue.
Build: burly; could run to fat. Spec.
peculiarities: scars on left knee due to surgery
for cartilage. Habits: moves and speaks slowly;
demeanour, quiet and reserved; drinks
sparingly; family man. Skills: radar expert,
good rifle shot. Religion: Presbyterian.
Education: Edinburgh Central School 1933–9;
Fettes College, Edinburgh 1939–46.
Professional: joined R.A.F. college Cranborne
in 1946; on to radar school 1949; into service
with V-bombers 1950; retired from R.A.F. in
1966; joined staff at Fylingdales 1966. Politics:
Liberal-Labour. Hobbies: carpentry; home
handyman.

PARENTS: John Henry Lawson, ship's chandler, born Edinburgh 1903. Died ... Helen, *née* Armstrong, housewife, born Edinburgh 1904. Died Edinburgh 1969.

GRANDPARENTS (paternal): John William Lawson, ship's chandler, born Edinburgh 1878. Died Edinburgh 1939. Margaret, *née* Drummond, housewife, born Edinburgh 1881. Died Edinburgh 1948.

GRANDPARENTS (maternal): Angus Armstrong, merchant seaman, born Portobello 1880. Died South Georgia, 1907. Alison, *née* Kirkwood, born Linlithgow 1883. Died Portobello, 1942.

SIBLINGS: brother George Lawson, ship's chandler, born Edinburgh 1936. Died ... sister Alison Lawson, private secretary, born Edinburgh 1939. Died ... brother, Angus Lawson, merchant seaman, born Edinburgh 1940. Died ...
Ends.

By the time we ground into York station at 10.57, dead on time, Charlie seemed satisfied at how much of the files we had committed to memory. Not pleased, but satisfied. As we crossed the wide, clean forecourt, he gave us our orders.

'Right,' he said. 'We'll split up. Get

18

yourselves a small suitcase each, and buy some gear. Don't be all day, and don't overdo it. Farrow, you hire a motor. Nothing fancy. We'll meet at the Hop Grove, a big boozer about two miles out on the Malton road. Right-hand side, impossible to miss it. You, Jock, take a taxi. All right?'

Charlie ducked into the hotel, presumably to walk straight through the lobby and out on the other side to check the car. Jock and I stepped out into the crisp spring sunshine, and the sheer beauty of York hit me just like it always does. We walked beside the wall as far as the river, crossed the bridge, and split up by the museum. Jock headed straight on towards the Minster, and I cut across into Davygate.

I used my credit card to buy a small suitcase, choosing a decent make. I needed one, and with a bit of luck old Charlie just might let me keep it. I had the usual trouble finding a shop which stocked size eighteen in shirts, but the socks and underwear were easy. I wondered briefly if I could get away with a pair of shoes, and decided no. I didn't overdo it, but I didn't buy any rubbish either. My shopping spree ran away with twenty minutes, and I'd an uncomfortable vision of Charlie waiting already out at the Hop Grove and wondering what the hell was keeping me. A friendly policeman told me where I could hire a car, and I hurried across Parliament Street to the garage in

19

Piccadilly. I chose a fairly new dark blue Cortina. The paperwork seemed endless, and the stolid Yorkshire car-hire manager didn't much like doing business with a credit card. They never do. I saw him in the rear-view mirror watching me take off towards the cattle market. He was rubbing his chin, and frowning dubiously.

I skirted the city centre on the road which runs beside the canal, crossed the bridge at Heworth Green, and hit the wide Malton Road doing over the limit. It was ten to twelve, and the local law seemed less fearsome than the waiting Charlie. Sure enough the Rover was there, rear-up to the saloon-bar door. It looked like the same car, and as I locked the Cortina I did a little mental sum to determine if it possibly could be. Maybe, but it was not important.

The saloon was busy, but not full. Charlie and Jock were sitting at a table in the corner. I got myself a pint of Tetley's at the bar and walked over to join them. Charlie took a long look at my pint pot, and I glanced quickly at his grapefruit juice. Christ, I thought, that's all we need! Jock was having what appeared to be a small Scotch. I took a pull at the pint, and sat down. Charlie nodded.

'Got the car?'

I nodded back. 'A Cortina. In good nick.'

'Right, then,' he said. 'Fylingdales first stop.

20

You know the way?'

'Yes,' I said. 'Straight up through Malton, on to Pickering, then head for Whitby. Decent roads, near enough forty miles. Let's say about fifty minutes.'

'Good. They're waiting for us, so let's get on with it. You can lead. Jock, you ride with me and I'll brief you *en route*.'

I picked up my pint, but Charlie was already moving. Jock tossed his whisky down, but I had no chance. I wanted that ale, and thought about it half the way to Malton. Charlie stuck hard on my tail, pushing me and the Cortina to the limit. Malton town slowed us down a bit, and my fifty minutes were up by the time we were clear of Pickering. We hurtled north over the moors, me with my foot flat on the floor.

The three great radomes loomed up suddenly, towering over the moors like enormous green golf balls. As we topped a rise, I could see the massive block-like buildings on which they were perched. Soon, a large sign told anyone who might still be in doubt about it that this was R.A.F. Fylingdales, and that all unauthorised persons had better keep the hell away. I swung the Cortina off the highway on to the access road, and pulled over with my nearside wheels in the heather to let Charlie precede me to the fortified gate in the high chainlink fence. He got out, and talked for a minute or two with the Air Force sergeant from the guardhouse. The sergeant shouted something at his men on the gate, and we passed into the most closely guarded thousand acres in Britain.

We were stopped again at the mouth of the tunnel which is the only way in to, or out of, the station proper. The tunnel starts a good mile from the first of the three station buildings, connects each one, and continues a mile beyond. Charlie got us into the thing, and we drove a mile along the curving neon-lit tube to an underground parking space. A worried-looking Flying Officer was waiting there to give us a smart salute. He led us up steps and along corridors and into what seemed like some sort of operations room. It was in a small office, just off this room, that we met the boss. Group Captain C. S. Hillier, D.F.C. Charlie established his own seniority by doing the introductions.

Hillier got right down to it, and my Fleet Air Arm man's opinion of what we used to call the Brylcreem Boys went up a notch. He was the sort of small man you think of afterwards as being big. About fifty. Not much hair left. His deep-set, very blue eyes drew one's gaze away from the white scar tissue which puckered the whole of one cheek and ran down his neck under his shirt collar. His grip was dry, and firm. Worry had made his face look old and grey. The Flying Officer took our coats, and

Hillier motioned to the three hard chairs ranged in front of his modest desk.

'Gentlemen,' he said, 'you are probably aware of the signals which have passed between myself and the Minister, so I won't go over old ground. But I want to tell you just enough about this place to make you aware of what we're up against.

'First, you can take it for fact that Fylingdales is absolutely impregnable to any interference from outside. The tunnel is the only way in. It's heavy steel, and the sections are married together by nearly a hundred miles of *hand-welded* joints. Do you know just what that means? Anyway, it brings me to the next bit.

'Anyone approaching the buildings by any other means than the tunnel would be fried to a crisp by the high-intensity radar beams before he'd got anywhere near. That's why we have the tunnel, and why the perimeter fence is so high and so far-reaching.

'The buildings are constructed in exactly the same way as the tunnel, and are overlaid with a thick shield of reinforced concrete. There are, of course, no doors and no windows. Nothing. In other words, the entire complex is one enormous, perfect—and I do mean perfect— seal. Are you with me?'

As we listened to him going on about the place, I began pretty quickly to see why it had cost over fifty million quid to build. God knows what it cost to run. A power station big enough to supply a town of sixty thousand, and all of the amenities necessary for the nurture and comfort of over a thousand people. Elaborate communications systems, stores, workshops, airmen's club, officers' mess, civilians' recreation centre, shops, hospital, guardrooms—the lot. I felt an urge to pull out an old envelope and start taking notes. Except, of course, that most of this was largely incidental. What it would all boil down to in the end was not the barrel itself but the quality of the apples. Charlie interrupted at what I had to admit seemed exactly the right time.

'That's fine, sir,' he said. 'Very useful. Now, what about the people? Any ideas of your own?'

The Group Captain passed a hand across his brow and squeezed his tired eyes. He sighed.

'I don't know. I just don't know. We kept the night shift here until about a couple of hours ago, then let them go home. There seemed no point in their hanging on. Besides, we never, for obvious security reasons, keep any more bods on the station than are necessary to run the thing. But I'm sure you've been briefed on all this. Seems to me—and I'm not just trying to pass the buck—that it's up to you chaps now. Would you like to see over the place?'

He took us on tour. The fantastic complex of radomes and computer rooms had a strange macabre beauty which was utterly and inexorably inhuman. All was deathly quiet. Only visible movement was that of the great radar dishes as they quested blindly and endlessly, up and down and back and forth, in the pale green twilight of their enormous patterned domes. We stood there like ants, and marvelled. In the computer room, serried banks of incredibly delicate machines worked without pause in a silence so eerie I could actually feel it in the roots of my tongue. Even the people, and there seemed remarkably few of them, made no noise. Hillier led us up and around and through and back, whispering his sales talk like a guide in a cathedral.

It was all very impressive but, like the Man said, there was no real point in our trying to take it in. I think Charlie just wanted to get the feel of the place. Anyway, he manoeuvred us out of it with what seemed almost like indecent haste, and we were soon back where the cars were parked. The Group Captain wished us luck. Charlie thanked him, and said we'd be in touch. We re-entered the tunnel and drove on through it to emerge far away on the north side. Charlie stopped the Rover on the narrow road between the tunnel exit and the perimeter fence, and they both got out. Jock slung his suitcase in the back of the Cortina, and got in after it. Charlie leaned on the door sill on my side.

'Listen,' he said, 'I want Jock under cover. Drop him somewhere near the railway station in Whitby, and he can get a taxi to the Royal. If we're here overnight, you stay there too. But you don't know each other. After you've dropped Jock, see Eldon and Chisholm. Put some pressure on. Don't pull any punches. Put the fear of Christ into them. I want a reaction. When you've done there, same thing with Sutcliffe down in Robin Hood's Bay. Understand?' I nodded, and he looked down at his watch. 'I'm going back down to Pickering to see Kemp, then on to Scarborough for a go at Lawson. It's twenty minutes to two. I'll ring you at the Royal at half past six. You got that?'

'What,' I asked sarcastically, 'about lunch?'

Charlie looked at me without expression. 'Lunchtime is past,' he said.

Before I could think of something scathing to counter with, he'd turned on his heel and was halfway back to the Rover. They let us out through the fence, and I waved to Charlie as he turned away south. If he saw me, he made no sign. Jock chuckled.

'You're wasting your time, boy,' he said. 'Charlie's a humourless bugger, even when he's relaxed. Not, mind you, that anybody's ever *seen* him relaxed. Jesus!' He clutched at his seat as I slammed the Cortina around and past a chap in a Morris Oxford doing fifty. The beat-up Jag coming the other way missed us by

26

almost an inch. 'We're not in that much of a rush!'

'Oh yes, we are.' I grinned at him, and kept my foot hard down. 'I know I can get to Whitby before the pubs close, but I'm not so sure about the fish shops. And I want some fish and chips even more than I want a pint. So hold on to your britches!'

But I couldn't see a fish and chip shop, and I knew there was no time to hunt around. So I settled, after I'd dropped Jock, for a couple of pork pies and a pint. The pies tasted all right, because I was hungry, but the pint was disappointing. In Tetley country they wouldn't have given it belly-room. I supped up without relish and asked the landlord how to get to Saddler's Rise.

Hilltop Avenue was a neat terrace of biggish stone houses with grey slate roofs and dormer windows. The pavements outside were washed and scoured, the different shades of scouring stones marking the boundaries of each household. Number 23 had pure white hand-crocheted curtains, now rare, and a doorstep worn hollow not so much by feet as by scrubbing. I knocked, and the door was opened eventually by a short, grey-haired woman in a plain Marks dress and a clean wrap-over pinafore. Elsie Fairbairn, widow, age sixty-two. Husband, Edward Fairbairn, coxswain for eleven years of the Whitby lifeboat, lost at sea

27

1963. Etcetera. It was all in the files.

'Mrs. Fairbairn?'

'That's right.' She had a ready smile. 'Can I help you?'

'Well,' I said, 'I'd like to see Mr. Eldon. Is he about?'

She covered her mouth with a hand on which, I noticed, the wedding ring was deep-embedded. 'Oh, I'm sorry, lad,' she said. 'You've missed him. It's his week-end off, and he's gone home to his grandma's. She lives in Oldham, you know. Manchester way.'

'Yes, I know,' I said. 'But never mind. I'll see him later. Is Mr. Chisholm in, then?'

Her face registered understanding. 'Oh,' she said, 'you must be from the radar. Yes, James is in—but I think he's asleep. He went up to his room when he'd had his dinner, said he was going to bed. He's been on nights, you know.'

'Yes, I know,' I said again. 'But it's right important. Can I come in?'

I saw Chisholm in Mrs. Fairbairn's front parlour. The room looked as though it had been cleaned especially for the job. The furniture was old, but sturdy and good. Everything smelled of polish. Chisholm came down in slacks and sweater, his thick reddish hair a tangle of uncombed locks. He wasn't tall, but he sure looked strong. The file had him dead to rights.

'Well, now,' he stopped just inside the door,

one hand still on the knob, 'and what can I do
for you?'

'You can come in and shut the door.'

'Oh, aye?' he said mildly. 'And who says so?'

'This says so.'

I let him see what said so, and he shrugged
his heavy shoulders. He closed the door, and
came on in to sit in one of the easy chairs beside
the empty fireplace. He lifted his slippered feet,
one after the other, on to the glass top of Mrs.
Fairbairn's coffee table.

'Right, then,' he said. 'Let's get it over with.
I want to get back to bed.'

'You and me both, lad,' I said. I perched on
the arm of the solid old sofa. 'So just tell us how
and why you did it.'

'What the hell d'you mean, why *I* did it?'

He looked so shocked and incredulous that I
almost hated to go on. But he didn't do any
knuckle-cracking, and that worried me. I gave
him the calm treatment.

'Sonny,' I said, 'somebody pulled the plug
out last night, and we know it was you. So get it
off your chest.'

His hands came together, then dragged
themselves apart. He ran them through his hair.

'Now look,' he said. 'All I know is that there
was a malfunction. Christ, it had to happen
some time! Why blame me?' He got belligerent.
'What the hell do you know about radar,
anyway?'

'Nothing.' I stood over him and pointed a

29

stiff finger right between his wide brown eyes. 'But we know a hell of a lot about *you*, Chisholm. So bloodywell out with it!'

He broke down then and cracked a knuckle. But that was all he cracked. I kept the pressure on for another ten minutes, then left him with his thoughts. I told him he was suspended from classified duties at Fylingdales, but to report for work as usual. Also, that if he tried to leave Whitby, he wouldn't get five yards. He threatened to see a lawyer, and I told him to feel free. I looked up as I ducked into the car, and saw him step back from the window.

I stopped at a roadside telephone booth on the way down to Robin Hood's Bay and rang Mr. Harris at the Royal Hotel. I told him that I'd failed to locate the first customer, as he was away visiting his firm's branch in Oldham. I said I'd been successful with the second one, though, and was on my way to contact the third. He just laughed.

Hannah Drake, Sutcliffe's landlady, was an older version of Mrs. Fairbairn. A little greyer, a little plumper. A little better off. There was a telephone on the table in the tiny hall of her neat brick-built bungalow, and the furniture in the front room was good reproduction. The spotless house was filled when I called with the delicious aroma of fresh-baked bread.

'Sit you down,' she said. 'I've just mashed a pot of tea. Would you like some? Do you have a cup, or a mug?'

'Lovely,' I said. 'I'll have a mug, please.'

I sat down, wondering if I dare hope. It was my lucky day. She came back with the tea and a big plate of cut and buttered currant tea-cakes. They were still warm enough to soften the chunkily spread butter. Mrs. Drake poured steaming tea into a mug for me, a cup for herself. It is not nice for women to drink out of mugs. I forced myself to take it easy with the tea-cake.

'I don't really know how long Harold's going to be,' she said. 'Sometimes, if he's having a good day, he just forgets what time it is.'

'What made him take his boat out today, then?' I said. 'Doesn't he usually go to bed when he gets home from work?'

'Oh, no,' Mrs. Drake shook her head, 'not always. It just depends. He's off tomorrow and Monday, you see, so he'll likely stop up now till about ten or eleven. Then he'll have a long lie in t'morning.'

I took the last piece of tea-cake. I couldn't help it. The old lady beamed.

'Could you eat some more?'

'No, thanks,' I lied. 'That was lovely. I wonder if it *is* worth waiting for him. Did he go with anybody?'

'I don't think so. But I'm not right sure. He got a phone call soon after he came home. Somebody ringing to tell him there was a run of spring haddock, he said. He didn't even wait to have a bite of dinner. I filled him a flask, and made him a sandwich, and he was off.'

'Did he say who it was had phoned him?'

'No, he didn't. He just got changed, and went down to get his boat out. If it's urgent, why don't you go down and see if you can see him? He might have got back already and be talking to Sam Mossop down at t'harbour...'

She told me how to get down to the harbour, and said I was welcome to come back with Sutcliffe for my tea.

The narrow road down to the little harbour gave me my first real sight of the sea. It looked almost blue in the brave spring sunshine, and the tops of the swell were whipped off white in the freshening breeze. I ran the car along the front and on to the little mole which protected the boats from the worst of the weather. The tide was well turned, and several converted whalers were lying askew in the mud close up under the wall. At the end of the mole, three men were unloading a coble called the *Yorkshire Lass* of its catch of shark-like dogfish. Watching them work, hands in the pockets of his corduroy trousers, was a short stocky man in an old flat cap and well-patched gumboots. If Mrs. Drake was any good at description, this must be Sam Mossop.

'Mr. Mossop?'

He took the old pipe out of his mouth and

leaned forward to spit over the edge of the jetty. His ancient eyes, set in a mass of weathered wrinkles, quizzed me narrowly.

'That's right, lad,' he said. 'An' what can I do for *thee*?'

I told him I'd just come from Mrs. Drake's, and was looking for Harold Sutcliffe.

'Aye, well,' he said, 'I think tha might 'ave a bit on a wait. Young Fred here'—he gestured with the stem of his pipe to one of the men down in the coble—'saw him as they were comin' in. He war well out. So he'll be a good hour yet, even if he's on his way back now.'

We both looked out to sea. There were a few small boats fairly close, and out on the bay another big coble heading in. I just assumed that if any of the small boats had been Sutcliffe's, Mossop would have known it and said so. I hesitated, undecided what to do. Mossop pointed to the incoming coble.

'Why doesn't tha wait and 'ave a word wi' . . . Hey! Ho'd on!'

The coble had altered course slightly for its run in, and was no longer bows-on to us. As it swung to starboard, we could see that it had something in tow. A bobbing dinghy, its motor hauled inboard and sticking up over the stern. Old Mossop shaded his eyes against the lowering sun.

'That's young Harold's boat,' he said. 'He must 'ave broken down, or summat, an' got

33

Fred Gilchrist to tak' him in tow. Anyway, he won't be long as he's in now.'

We stood waiting for the second coble to enter the little harbour and come alongside. Old Mossop talked about Sutcliffe as though he were a favourite son. I heard what a grand lad he was. That, although he'd got brains he wasn't 'brussen'. Didn't sup much, but would always have a gill or a shandy, even if it was only the one. Liked his bit of fishing, and was a fair hand at it. Kept just enough from his catches to do himself and Mrs. Drake, and gave the rest away. Left it with Billy Barnforth at the Tiger. Billy kept the fish in a barrel of ice in his cellar, and gave it to anyone who asked. Mostly pensioners and such. Bay folk were not right good at taking to strangers, even other Yorkshiremen, but young Harold had made a hit right from the start.

The coble wallowed past the end of the mole, and we watched it come in. It eased slowly alongside, and a big young man in cracked yellow oilskins leaped from the gunwale and threw a couple of turns around the bollard. The ungainly boat ground its old motor-car-tyre fenders against the worn stones of the jetty, and I looked down into the dinghy bobbing under its stern. Apart from a battered red vacuum flask, a few mackerel, and about a dozen good haddock flopping weakly under the thwarts, it was empty. The man in the tiny wheelhouse cut the diesel motor and hurried, clumsy in his seaboots, to cross the little deck. He scrambled up on to the jetty and caught the arm of one of the several small boys who had appeared out of nowhere to watch the boat come in.

'Listen, Davy,' he said urgently. 'Run up t'police station an' tell Sergeant Easeman to come down right away. Tell 'im Mester Gilchrist said so. Go on, lad—hurry up!'

The three men unloading the ugly, bloody fish from the other coble left off and came over to see what was going on. As the boy sped on his way, old Mossop put a hand on the sleeve of Gilchrist's oilskin coat.

'What's up, Ernest?' he said. 'An' where's young Harold?'

Gilchrist looked around our circle of enquiring faces. His own was grim. He wiped his lips with the back of a horny hand, and shook his head. 'There's been an accident, Sam,' he said hoarsely. 'We spotted Harold's dinghy about four mile out. Then we spotted *him*. Kept afloat by 'is oilskins, I reckon. We pulled 'im inboard, and our Keith tried t'kiss o' life. But he war too far gone. He's lyin' over yonder on t'port side.'

I jumped down on to the coble's deck. Sutcliffe's body was lying on its back behind the little deckhouse, head on one side and eyes closed. His broken nose looked white and pinched, and his lips were an ugly grey.

Otherwise he could have been asleep. The short dark hair clung to his head in wet tendrils. I squatted beside him and lifted his clenched right hand. Wrapped so tightly around his palm that it bit into the flesh was a length of strong line. The end in his fist was neatly whipped, the other end was broken off raggedly at about eighteen inches.

Both Gilchrists had stepped into the boat after me, and the father tapped me on the shoulder.

'Here, I say,' he said. 'Who are *you*, mester? This is a job for t'police, you know. You can't . . .'

'That's all right.' I straightened up, and let him see the jotter. 'Are you sure this is Harold Sutcliffe?'

'Sure?' He took off his cap and scratched the weathered top of his bald head. 'O' course, I'm sure!'

I looked at Gilchrist junior, standing up against the boxlike wheelhouse. He nodded. 'Oh aye, it's Harold all right,' he said. He shook his head slowly. 'Poor bugger.'

'Either of you got any ideas as to how it could have happened?'

Tom glanced at his father for a lead. The older fisherman shrugged his heavy shoulders. 'Hard to say,' he said. 'But tha can see how t'line's cut into his hand. Happen he got a mackerel on, an' summat big took a snatch at it.

36

Pulled him over t'side...'

'Something big? What would that be?'

'Well, I don't rightly know,' Old Gilchrist had another go at his head, and looked for help from his son. '*Could* 'ave been a dolphin, or summat of that sort. If Harold war leanin' over, off balance, it *might* 'ave toppled him out...'

'You don't seem to fancy the idea, though,' I said.

'Nay,' he replied, 'it only comes to mind because there's nowt else it *could* be. We've had no weather. There's been nobbut a little swell all day. *Summat* must 'ave pulled 'im out. Besides I reckon he must 'ave taken a knock as he went over. Else why didn't he swim for it? Harold war a fair swimmer—wasn't he, Tom?'

Tom shrugged again. 'Well,' he said. 'I know he could swim. Just 'ow *good* he war, I wouldn't like to say...'

The men from the *Yorkshire Lass* were crouched on their hunkers at the edge of the jetty, taking it all in. I looked up at the one I thought was the skipper. Him with the grizzled whiskers, who wore his cap pulled back to front.

'I hear you saw him as you were coming in,' I said. 'What time would that be?'

Instead of answering, he looked at Mossop. The old man took his pipe out. 'An hour or two back,' he said. 'Must ha' been fowerish. Aye, about fower o'clock.'

I tried the old skipper with another one. 'What sort of luck was he having?' I nodded down at the haddock in the dinghy bottom. 'Had he got this lot when you saw him?'

This time I got an answer.

'No, mester,' the old man said. 'He 'ad not. He'd nobbut a few mackerel then. He must 'ave come on t'haddock later on, like ...'

I looked at my watch. Ten to six. So Sutcliffe had found himself a school of haddock, baited his hand lines and taken over a dozen good fish, fallen overboard, drowned, been sighted, picked up and brought ashore—all in the space of two hours. A fit, strong boy. An athlete in training. I didn't like it. I bent over to look at his head. So far as I could see, there was no bruise or abrasion anywhere. I asked old man Gilchrist just one more question.

'Any other boats about when you picked him up?'

He pursed his salt-cracked lips. 'No,' he said, 'not nigh on. We did see one or two of the usual silly buggers up from Scarboro' ...' He looked up suddenly across the bay. A raucous motor boat bounced along the top of the swells, its painted nose jutting skywards and the wash from its powerful engine spreading fan-like in its wake. '... There's one on 'em now. But nothin' else, not close enough to 'elp ...'

The pale blue Morris 1000 had a police sign on its roof. I got back up on to the jetty and caught the sergeant as he was heaving himself out of the driving seat. I told him who I was, and proved it. He sat back in, and leaned over to unlatch the nearside door. I got in with him.

'What's up?' he said. 'Have we got trouble?'

I told him we had, and that it was a damned sight bigger than both of us. I asked him to have Sutcliffe's body taken somewhere safe, and watched carefully until he got further instructions. The dinghy too. He seemed an efficient sort of chap, and said I could depend on him. I told him we'd be in touch very soon.

I took the Cortina up on to the Whitby road and stopped at the first call box. The idiot on the hotel switchboard finally put me through to Jock's room, just in time for the pips to start chattering. I stuck in another tanner, and got Jock before he hung up. I told him the number of the box I was in, and asked him to call me back. The sun was down, and the evening had turned chill. I stamped my feet on the concrete floor and waited for Jock to leave the hotel and find himself a phone booth of his own. When he came on, I told him the story. He didn't interrupt me more than a couple of dozen times throughout. When I was finished, he whistled.

'What d'you think?'

'I think he was done. What do *you* think?'

'I think you could be right. Look, I've got to get back for the contact with Charlie. You'd better come in. Nothing more you can do down there. See you at the hotel in about fifteen minutes.'

When I walked into the Royal, Jock was standing at the reception desk. He appeared to be paying his bill. I went past him into what they called the cocktail bar. The elderly barmaid tore herself away from her *Yorkshire Evening Post* and delved among her stock of bottles for one of Canadian Club. She seemed surprised when she found it, but told me that ice was no problem. I ordered a double. Jock came in and took the stool next to mine. I let him buy his own. When the barmaid moved away to serve someone else, I stuck a pipe in my mouth and asked Jock if he had a match.

'Bloody brilliant,' he said softly. 'Where's the car?'

I told him it was round the corner. He said to get it, and to meet him where I'd dropped him on the way in. I told him I was hungry.

'Sorry,' he said. 'I'm a stranger here myself. Perhaps this lady can help...'

I asked the barmaid how to get to the fish dock and was glad, when she was through telling me, that I didn't need to get there. I supped up and left. Jock joined me at the rendezvous about ten minutes later. He slung his suitcase into the back, and got in beside me.

'Charlie wants us to meet him down at Pickering,' he said. 'He'll pick us up just this side of town. We'll need to watch out for him.'

'Bloody marvellous.' I let in the clutch. 'And when are we supposed to eat? My belly thinks my throat's been cut.'

'Courage, lad,' he grinned. 'Think what a fine job we're doing.'

We shot over twenty miles of moor in just about as many minutes. The Rover was parked in a lay-by two miles north of town. Jock spotted it in time for me to brake hard and pull in behind. Charlie had seen us coming up, and was into the back seat before I'd time to switch off the engine.

'Now, then,' he said. 'What's this about Sutcliffe?'

I told him all I knew. He interrupted only twice: once to confirm that Mrs. Drake had no other lodgers, and again to make sure that she hadn't known who telephoned Sutcliffe with the message about the run of haddock.

'What do you think about Chisholm? Did you give him a fright?'

'I tried,' I said, 'but he's not the type who scares easy. If he *is* our man, we've got a job on. What about your chums?'

Charlie leaned forward, knuckles together and forearms stretched across the seat backs.

'I don't know,' he mused. 'Lawson seems all right, but I wouldn't put it past young Kemp. One of these stroppy little buggers. A sodding intellectual. I'm a long way from being done with him yet.'

Jock coughed. I think he was feeling a bit guilty at having had nothing, so far, to do. 'Well, what now?' he said. 'Do we go back and look into the Sutcliffe job?'

'No, Jock.' Charlie shook his head. 'A waste of time. We'll leave that to the local coppers. They're doing a post mortem right now. If Sutcliffe died from anything else but drowning, we'll know before the night's out. No, I think you two better get across to Huddersfield. I want to know more about the families. You, Jock, get after Eldon. Scare him. Let him know he's suspended, and he's to stay where he is until we tell him otherwise. Watch what he does.'

'What about transport?' I said. 'We've only got one car.'

Charlie looked up at me, and the headlights from a passing bus glinted on his rimless specs. 'You shouldn't need a motor. But if you do, you'll just have to hire one. Get everything you can on Sutcliffe and Chisholm, but concentrate on Chisholm. Any questions?'

We made our contact arrangements, and I swung the Cortina out of the lay-by as Charlie was ducking into the Rover. I liked him even less than before, but maybe that was just because I was hungry. I asked Jock what about stopping in Pickering for something to eat, and he said no because we might run into Charlie. I told him what, for all I cared, could happen to

Charlie, but pushed the Cortina straight on through town and out on to the Malton Road. We stopped there at the Green Man and I had ox-tail soup, rump steak with everything, a double helping of treacle dumpling, and Stilton cheese with two hard rolls. Coffee in a breakfast cup. Jock watched me at my muttons, and said he wondered where the hell I was putting it all.

My pipe lasted right through York, and I turned west on the road to Leeds feeling a good deal better than I had all day. I risked the city centre rather than trek all the way round the ring road, and struck lucky with a lull in the traffic. Soon we were well out of town and pulling up the long hill past the Pack Horse. Jock's head started to nod, and soon dropped on to his chest. His gentle snores accompanied me over the dark miles to Huddersfield, and I woke him in St. George's Square. As he slid over into the driving seat, I got my new suitcase out of the boot. He wound his window down.

'Right, Jock,' I said, 'you're on your own. I'll book in here, at the George. If you're going to Oldham over Nont Sarah's Way, watch yourself!' I grinned down at him. 'Don't forget what happened to me!'

I watched him pull away, then turned back wearily towards the lights of the George. It was ten minutes to eleven, and drizzling. If they'd said there were no rooms, I might quite easily have wept. But Saturday night is usually easy, and I had no trouble. I remember getting undressed, and I remember dropping into bed. What I don't remember is thinking what a hell of a long, hard day it had been.

SUNDAY

Chisholm's grandmother reminded me very much of my own. She lived in one of a row of old stone houses set in a narrow dirt yard. Opposite, majestic in its awfulness, the tall end wall of a carpet mill kept the yard in almost perpetual shadow. People in School Street had to keep their houses lit the whole day. Gay print curtains and clean-scoured flagstones were weapons in a battle that was grim and eternal.

Getting the old lady to talk was no trouble at all. Once I assured her that Jimmy 'wasn't in any bother', she seemed glad of the chance. She told me how her husband had gone off and got himself killed in the Spanish Civil War, and how, if he'd been old enough at the time, her son Jesse would have gone with him.

Politics. It was all to do with politics. She herself could never understand the half of what it was they were always on about. Not that Jesse's being too young to go with his dad had spared him for long. He was taken in the next lot, anyway. Now, with Jesse's wife killed on

44

her holidays a few years back, all she had left was her grandson. But he was a grand lad, and a great comfort. Funny, she thought he would be home this weekend. Happen she was getting mixed up. It might be his work. He had a good job, and was doing right well at it. Would I like a sup of tea?

I told her no thanks, that it hadn't been long since my breakfast. Off she went again in her rocking chair, wrinkled hands clasped across her clean pinafore. We faced each other across the massive black-leaded fireplace with its hob on one side and its oven on the other. The big room was straight old Yorkshire, kitchen sink in the corner beside the window, big square table draped now by a plush cover with bobbled fringe. The television set behind my chair and next to the sideboard looked oddly out of place. Set into the cheap oval mirror over the cluttered mantelpiece was a badly coloured portrait photograph of a young man in naval uniform. He looked a lot like James, so was possibly the father. The old lady caught me looking up at it, and sighed.

'That's him,' she said. 'That's our Jesse—and that,' she pointed to a framed likeness on the mantelshelf of a fair-haired woman, 'is Jimmy's mam. Our Jesse's wife, poor lass.'

'Yes,' I said, 'it was an accident, wasn't it? Somewhere in Germany?'

'No, lad. Austria. She *war* a German,

though, you know. Come over here just before t'war started. Her mam and dad war murdered, like, in one of them camps. I never could understand what she wanted to keep on going back for. If it had been me, I'd a' kept well away...'

'Did she go back a lot, then?'

'Oh, aye!' the old lady nodded emphatically. 'They went every year for their holidays. Never missed once.'

'They? I thought you said she was on her own?'

'Well, yes, she was on her own that last time. But our Jimmy war allus with her afore that. He talks German, an' all, you know.' Mrs. Chisholm shook her white head. 'I *telled* her she shouldn't go on her own. I *telled* her...'

Her round Yorkshire accents rolled on and on, but I was only half listening. She rambled away, not even pausing when I got up and pokered the fire. Something which, in someone else's house, you just don't do. I sat down again and caught her just as she was describing her late daughter-in-law's evening job as barmaid down at the Polish Club on Wakefield Road.

'Did you say Polish Club?'

'Oh, aye,' she hardly paused. 'She spent a lot of time down there, you know. Well, they're summat the same, aren't they, Poles and Germans? I mean, they both come from over yonder. Our Jimmy used to go down sometimes

46

and help her. He still does go down, now and again. Well, our Ilse worked there for a long time. Nearly since it started...'

One of the instructors at the big house in Sutherland had told us once that in our business hunches were just about as much real use as a monkey's left knacker. Better, always, to take proper heed of the *facts*. Well, the *fact* was, sitting there listening to that old lady, I was assailed by the biggest most persistent hunch of my fairly hunch-less life. Then something Mrs. Chisholm went on to say jerked me out of my reverie. She was back on the subject of her son.

'...a lad from Ossett. Lovely young feller, he was. Fancy him being on t'same ship. You wouldn't credit it, would you?'

She was talking about a shipmate of her son's, someone who had come to see her afterwards. The name had rung a bell.

'Lumb? Did you say Lumb?'

'Aye, that's it. Lumb. Gawthorpe feller. Near Ossett, you know. Where they used to have t'Maypole Feast. I can't rightly remember his first name...'

But I could. It had to be Edwin. Big Ned Lumb. Played second row for Wakefield Ramblers when I was a full back for St. Helens. We'd clashed hard in more than one match, and done some hard drinking together afterwards. Ned never did much talking about his Navy days. What I knew, I'd heard from others. He went down with the *Glasgow*, and was picked up three days later. Two straight years then in Russian convoys, in minesweepers. Three times sunk and once, off the *Gleaner*, the only survivor. Last I heard he was working six shifts a week down the pit and, at about forty-eight years old, still turning out with Wakefield to play the toughest game in the world.

I let the old lady talk for another ten minutes or so, then left her with her burgeoning memories. Outside, a brave shaft of sunlight struck the precise angle at which it could pass the corner of the mill. It fell, like a finger of God, on to a cracked flagstone. I walked back to the George, wondering how I could get hold of Ned Lumb.

The dark blue Cortina was parked in Northumberland Street. I almost passed it. But the registration number checked, and so did our mark. I looked around for lurking coppers or nosy citizens, then let myself in. If I'd waited just a couple of minutes, old Jock would have been there to open the door with the key. He came up quickly, and got in beside me.

'Surprise,' he grinned. 'I've just left a message for you at the George.'

'Where's Eldon?' I said.

'Gone back to Whitby. Had a bust-up last night with his girl friend, and buggered off back in a huff. Must have passed us, going the other way. I've been in touch with Charlie. He said to leave Eldon to him, and carry on here with you. What have you got?'

I told him what I'd learned from Mrs. Chisholm, and asked him what he thought. He thought the same as I did. That I should go and see Mrs. Sutcliffe, then try to contact Ned Lumb. He said he would book in at the Queen's, and we fixed to meet up at the Three Nuns for a late lunch. He got out, and I drove on past him to run round the square and out along Kirkgate towards the Wakefield Road.

The slag-heaps of Barnsley loomed on the windscreen just after eleven o'clock, and I ran out over Moortop. The little house in Warner's Fold had its curtains drawn. That meant they knew. I imagined the scene inside, and almost flunked it. The door was opened by a big young woman whose resemblance to Sutcliffe was unmistakable. Her handsome face was creased with grief.

'Miss Sutcliffe?' I cleared my throat to make way for the lie. 'I'm from the police.'

'Oh . . . yes,' she stood back from the door, 'of course. Yes, come in.'

The room was very hot. Some people have garbage shutes. Others have waste-disposal units. The families of Yorkshire miners keep big fires burning, winter and summer. The old lady sitting in the straight-backed wooden armchair by the roaring grate seemed to feel the heat not at all. She looked up dully as I came in,

49

first at me, then at her daughter. Her wrinkled face was grey with fatigue. They must have been told last night. The younger woman took my raincoat.

'It's about our Harold again, Mam,' she said gently. 'Are you all right, love?'

Mrs. Sutcliffe's sigh seemed to pull at my throat. I looked down at the hand-pricked rug in front of the fire-place. *Father: Herbert Sutcliffe, miner, born Barnsley, Yorks., 1920. Died (mine accident) 1963. Brother, Albert Sutcliffe, born Barnsley, Yorks., 1945. Died (mine accident) 1963.* Jesus. Both of them, and probably together. Now the other son. The one they had scrimped and scraped and gone without for. To send him to college and a better, safer life. I had a sudden mind's-eye picture of him lying there on the cold wet deck of the coble. I sat down without being asked.

'What is it now, lad? I thought we'd telled you everything already...'

I did not impose long. I just hadn't the heart for it. Whilst I was talking to the old lady, Sutcliffe's sister went into the sink corner and put the kettle on. She broke in to ask if I'd like a drink of tea. I told her it was very kind, but that I was a bit late already. I left them to their suffering as soon as I decently could, glad to get away.

I drove back into Wakefield, found an un-vandalised phone box, and looked in the tattered directory for Walmsley, L. N. There were three of them, but I was right first time. Ten to twelve. I kept my fingers crossed as I got the ringing tone, hoping I'd caught him before he was gone for his Sunday pint.

'Who? Marcus Farrow? Oh aye! Well hello, old lad! How are you getting on? Are you still laking at football?'

I told him I'd given up playing rugby, and he told me he was still managing Wakefield. I asked him then if he could give me Ned Lumb's address.

'Nay, I can't, lad. He's moved now. Lives somewhere round Earlsheaton. Any road, he wouldn't be in. He does a bit of trainin' on Sunday mornings. He still lakes for us, tha knows. Plays hell when he's picked for t'second team, an' all! Still, we've got to make room for t'young uns . . .'

I said that was right, but I had to see Ned, and how did he think I could get hold of him. He told me to ask at Earlsheaton Lowside Club. I thanked him, and promised to look him up next time I was in Wakefield.

Earlsheaton is a district of Dewsbury, grim black pearl of the heavy woollen district. It looks down from the top of a long steep hill on to the grimy town centre in the valley bottom. The working men's club sits between the two, perched on a broad ledge in the hillside. Access is by a precarious single-track road paved

51

haphazardly with old stone boulders. I eased the Cortina down over the murderous bumps, and inched it on to the tiny dirt car park.

The white-whiskered old man on the door would not let me in. I wasn't a member, and I wasn't affiliated. Then I told him I was looking for Ned Lumb, and everything was suddenly all right. He signed me in himself, said he hadn't seen Ned yet, but to go on in and have a pint. Ned was sure to be in directly.

There is something very special about the atmosphere in working men's clubs. It is warm and friendly and entirely unpretentious. The one on Lowside was typical of all the others I had ever seen. The older ones, that is. A single barn-like room with a long bar at one end, and two beautifully kept snooker tables smack in the middle. Horse-hair-covered bench seats all the way round the walls, fronted by heavy little tables on cast-iron pedestals. That lovely smell of beer. It was early, but both snooker tables were already in use. They would be now until three o'clock closing.

There were no women in the place, not even behind the bar. Not at dinner-time. I got a pint of ale and a penny change for my tenpenny piece, and sat down to watch the snooker: The beer was Webster's, not Tetley's, but it was quite well kept and not at all bad. I got a pipe going, my first of the day. Life began to take on a certain comfort.

Most men who know him will tell you that Ned Lumb is as big as the side of a house. Of course, he is not. He only seems as big. The steward at the door must have told him he'd a visitor, because he paused just inside the door and looked around. He had changed very little. But his hair was largely gone, and the top of his head was pitted with the hard blue scars that are the marks of a miner's trade. Then he saw me across the room, and his homely face split into the wide familiar grin.

'Well, bugger me! Bloody old Marcus, lad! What brings thee over this way?'

He got himself a pint, and a gill in mine to top it up, and we moved to a table in the corner. We talked for a while about football—in the West Riding there is only one kind of *football*—and I tried then to work the conversation around to Navy days. Ned was reluctant as always to talk about his time in the service, and I was forced in the end to come right out with it.

'Look, Ned. This is important. I can't say much about why, but I want you to tell me everything you can remember about Jesse Chisholm. All right?'

He turned his head to look at me, saw how serious I was, then nodded. He leaned forward, elbows on knees, watching the snooker players as they moved around the tables. After a few moments he began to talk.

'Well,' he said slowly, 'there's not a right lot to tell. I didn't know him all that well. None of us did. He used to keep to hisself, like. He war a funny bloke, in a way . . .'

Ned and Chisholm had been shipmates on the *Reaper*, a fleet minesweeper, for just over eight months. Ned had been a Leading Seaman and Chisholm a Sparks—a radio operator working also on the sweeper's R.D.F. gear. During this time the *Reaper* had accompanied three convoys on the run to Murmansk. Then, in the summer of '43, they had tempted fate once too often. They were two days out of Methil on a clear calm night. The U-boats, a pack of them, struck with the usual absence of warning. Curiously, the *Reaper* took the first tin fish.

Ned was on watch, up on the bridge. He had seen the phosphorous wake of the torpedo brief seconds before it hit, and had yelled a warning. Then the whole ship disintegrated in an enormous belch of noise and fire, and he felt himself hurtling through a wall of upflung spray. He hit the water with a smack that knocked him almost senseless. The sea round him, bone-chilling as it was, seemed to boil. He surfaced in the middle of a patch of blazing oil and dove again, encumbered by his seaboots and oilskins, to strike out desperately away from it. When he came up again, the night was thunderous with the roar of exploding

54

munitions, and the sky all around was red with flames. Assorted chunks of superstructure were falling out of the sky like monstrous hail.

He heard a cry for help, and saw a head bobbing just yards away. It was Chisholm. One side of his skull was laid open by a four-inch gash, and pouring blood. Ned got a hold on him and towed him, God knows how, to a hunk of wreckage big enough to bear his weight. They managed between them to get Chisholm up on to it, then Ned let go to struggle out of his boots and oilskins. When he'd got them off, Chisholm had drifted away, lost in the troughs.

A couple of months later in the year, or a few hundred miles further north, and Ned's chances of survival for more than a few minutes would have been less than nil. As it was, he kept himself afloat for over four hours and was picked up at dawn by the *Vostock*, a Russian escort destroyer. He was transferred later that same day to the cruiser *Orion*, and stayed aboard her for the rest of the convoy. The *Reaper* had been a Chatham ship, and Ned learned on his return to the depot for further draft that he had been one of only five survivors. Chisholm was not among them. Ned had been granted seven days' leave, and that was when he had gone to see Chisholm's mother.

I got up to fetch us two more pints. The club had filled up, and the barmen were busy.

Whilst I was waiting to be served, I packed another pipe. When I got back, Ned was talking to a man with a coffee-coloured whippet. He was leaning forward on his seat, elbows on knees, to take the dog's fragile head between his great scarred hands. The little hound was shivering, as they always are, long bony tail tucked in tight under its narrow buttocks. Seeing that I was returning, the man, a big young miner, grinned shyly and moved away.

'So-long then, Ned. See tha int'morn.'

Ned nodded after them. 'Not a bad little dog, that. Won me a quid or two, she has.'

'Ned, listen,' I said. 'What was that about Chisholm being a bit funny?'

'Well, he *war* ... ' Ned frowned, groping for words. He wrapped a hand around his pint pot, and took a long pull at it. 'He war same as a bloody 'ermit. He had a bunk in t'wireless cabin, an' hardly ever moved out on it. Used to read a lot. *Big* books, tha knows. Heavy stuff. An' he used to go ashore reg'lar—on his own, an' all!'

I asked him what he meant, and he told me. Most matelots would take a first run ashore in Murmansk or Archangel, but once was usually enough. After that, they just stayed on board and caught up on their sleep. There was nothing to go ashore for. There was no Russian money, and even if there had been, there was nothing in the shops to buy. Besides, the Russians—especially the women—just didn't want to know. Even apart from the language difficulty, it was hopeless trying to talk to any of them. Bloody hopeless.

'What did Chisholm *do*, then?'

'Nay, lad,' Ned shook his head, 'God knows. He wouldn't have told us if we'd have asked him. He war a close-mouthed sod, all right. Poor bugger.'

Ned wanted me to go back home for 'a bit of dinner', but I said we'd have to leave it for another day. I was glad he didn't ask me what it was all about. I would have hated to lie to him. As it was, he came outside to see me into the Cortina. He admired the car without envy, although I knew he would probably never aspire to one of his own. I jolted up the narrow track, and shot down the hill into Dewsbury. The town centre was practically deserted. I skirted the town hall, took the road behind the bus station, and headed out towards Mirfield. I was at the Three Nuns, a great big roadside pub about two miles this side of Huddersfield, in just over ten minutes.

Jock had tipped the waitress to give us a table over in the corner, near a window. I told him about my morning over roast ribs of beef and Yorkshire pudding. The food was very good. Jock looked at his watch as the cheese arrived, and felt in his waistcoat pocket. He came up with a fistful of fivepenny pieces, and a twist of paper. He pushed the lot across the tablecloth towards the edge of my plate.

'Half past two. Time for you to ring Charlie. That's the number. Better use the phone box outside.'

Charlie picked his phone up at the first ring. When I started to tell him about my session with Mrs. Chisholm, he cut me short.

'I've heard that already, from Jock. How did you get on with the others?'

I told him what had passed at the Sutcliffe house, and most of my talk with Ned Lumb. When I'd finished, he was silent. I fed money into the coin box to give him time.

'You think the Russians picked up Chisholm, too?'

'I was wondering when you were going to ask me that.'

'This isn't funny, Farrow. What d'you think—yes or no?'

'How the hell would I know? How would anybody know? Ask me if it's possible I say yes, it is. Ned Lumb was picked up. So were others. So why not Chisholm?'

'Why not indeed ... ' Charlie began to make the low tuneless humming noise that I later came to know so well. I could just see him pushing his specs further up on his nose. I put more money in the box. He waited till the coins had stopped falling, then coughed.

58

'Farrow? How's your German?'

He knew damned well just exactly how my German was, almost to the word. I admitted to a fair smattering.

'Right. Listen. I want you to go to Kitzbuhel. Do some sniffing on the Ilse Chisholm thing...'

'You thinking what I'm thinking?'

'Very probably. Anyway, I want it checked out, and I want it checked out good. Now, here's the form...'

'Here, hold on a minute!' I'd suddenly thought of something. 'Tomorrow's Monday. I'm supposed to be at work...'

'You'll just have to go sick then, won't you? Haven't you got any holidays due?'

He waited for an answer, and my heart sank. I'd been looking forward to Scotland, and some long calm days of fishing the Earn. 'Well, I *do* have a spring week coming up, but...'

'But nothing.' Charlie's tone was mild. 'It's spring now, isn't it? Look, you know the Leeds and Bradford airport?' I said I did. 'Right, go back for your gear and be there'—a pause—'at six o'clock. Get Jock to take you. Tell him I said to look out for Sam Harvey. Oh, and by the way, no hardware. Got it?'

I told him I had, and he hung up. Just like that. What a terrible waste of fivepenny pieces. I rested the receiver a few seconds then dialled my sister's number in Bramhall. The ring was answered by her husband Brian, and I could hear the kids yelling in the background. He told me that Psyche was in the loo. I asked him to get her to phone the office first thing in the morning, tell them I'd been off colour over the weekend, and had decided to start my spring week forthwith. He said he would do that small thing, and started to ask me where I was. I said thanks very much, give my love to Psy and the kids, and did a Charlie on him.

Jock dropped me off at the George and I slept soundly in a chair in the deserted residents' lounge until he came back for me just before five. We hit Bradford over Odsal Top, and shot off to the right on the wide ring road out towards the airport at Yeadon. We got there with ten minutes to spare. Jock parked the Cortina by the airport buildings, and I got my suitcase out of the boot. There were one or two light aircraft warming up at dispersal points around the field and, a hundred yards away across the grass, a neat little blue-and-white jet was sucking fuel from a cow-like bowser. Jock cocked a thumb at it.

'There she is, laddie,' he grinned. 'Just for you. Make you feel important?'

'Makes me feel like I'm off on a bloody busman's holiday,' I said. We started walking out towards the plane. There was a fair old wind. 'Here—what about Customs?'

'Customs my arse,' Jock chuckled. 'We're all

working for the same government, aren't we? Let's get you aboard, before you start worrying about duty-free liquor!'

As we drew near, the rumbling bowser stowed its hoses and lurched away. The pilot, a fair-haired lad with merry blue eyes and a broken front tooth, slapped old Jock on the back and mock-punched him in the guts. He looked a lot too young.

'How's it hanging, you sporran-swinging haggis-scoffing bagpipe-bashing old bastard!' He turned to me, his arm still across Jock's shoulders. 'And who's this—your new keeper?'

'Pack it in, you silly young bugger. This here is Marcus Aurelius Farrow, and he's of a very nervous disposition. If he finds out you haven't passed your test on this thing he might make me take him back home to his mammy.'

The boy's grip was dry and firm. 'Hello, Mark,' he grinned. 'Sam Harvey. Don't worry about this barmy old sod. I *have* passed my test—he just hasn't heard about it yet. Anyway'—he looked at the many-dialled watch on his slim wrist—'we'd best be getting airborne. You made your will, and everything?'

The plane was a little beauty. A Hawker Siddeley 125. Twin Rolls-Royce Bristol Viper engines carried close to the fuselage, well aft of the cabin area. Inside, a lovely neat layout. Four luxurious seats, one on each side fore and aft, and between them two bunk-like divans.

Jock stuck his head in at the door, and held out his hand.

'Well, good luck, old son. See you tomorrow or the next day. Take care of yersel'!'

Sam started the engines on the batteries. The cabin lights dimmed, and there was a high keening noise. Then both Vipers fired with a coughing roar, and there was some small vibration as we bumped gently across the grass to take-off point. Sam had left the door to the flight deck wide open, and I could hear him asking the control tower for clearance. I strapped myself into the rear seat on the port side and peered out of the little window looking for Jock. He saw me, and gave me thumbs up.

We taxied out to the far edge of the field, and Sam slewed the plane round into the wind. He did his checks, and the engine note climbed to screaming pitch. The little plane seemed to stand on its tiptoes and dance in fury with its eagerness to be off. There was a rush of hydraulics as Sam released his brakes, and we were away. The 125 gained airspeed very quickly. We were well clear and climbing steeply in what seemed like a lot less than a thousand yards. The pressure of the seat against the small of my back was firm and comforting. We banked sharply at about seven thousand feet, then levelled off to settle on course. A few minutes later, Sam had set his gyro and was flying on auto. He ducked back into the cabin and tossed a large blue envelope into my lap.

'There's your bumf,' he said. 'Compliments of the boys in the back room. Delivered as per instructions, soon as airborne and flying on a true course.' He sank into the seat opposite. 'Well? Aren't you going to ask me if it's safe up here without a driver?'

'Get knotted, sonny. I was flying off ships when you were yelling for your Mammy to wipe your bottom.'

He just about knocked himself out laughing at that one, and I opened up my envelope. Inside was a well-worn passport, a postcard-size blow-up of a snapshot photograph showing an attractive fair-haired woman of around thirty-five, two typewritten sheets of instructions, and a bundle of Austrian currency notes to the value of five hundred schillings.

The passport was an exact duplicate of my real one except for the name and address and occupation. I was now William Thompson, Insurance Assessor, of 7, Wellesley Gardens, Manchester 6. I settled down to study the instructions.

Soon, the weather broke, and the little kite began to take a buffeting. Squalls of rain hammered at the fuselage, and we plunged into swirling cloud. Sam went up forrard to take the plane off George and try to get above the weather. I squeezed into the tiny kitchen and nosed around. There was even a drinks locker.

I helped myself to a decent Scotch, failed to find any ice, and drank it with plain water. Then I began to remember all I'd heard about the airport at Innsbruck, cocked an ear to the worsening storm, and decided that the situation merited another.

The Inn Valley is a long, narrow cleft in the Austrian Alps. On fine days it is beautiful, and passengers with strong nerves can watch the wing-tips scrape the shining peaks on either side with not much more than the occasional tremor. Unfortunately, the valley is subject to sudden violent storms. When these happen, or even threaten, the airport at Innsbruck is very firmly closed down. Which is why, in 1970, most civil airlines had stopped scheduling regular flights. The only way into Innsbruck airport is up the Inn Valley.

The stuff in the wind was a mixture of snow and rain. It battered against the 125 with deafening violence. Gale-force gusts tore at the mainplanes, and mountains yawned crazily all about us. I sat beside young Harvey in the co-pilot's seat, hands itching to take the dual controls and help him keep the little plane on an even keel. He was bent forward over the stick to peer through the swirling cloud, one eye on his instruments. So help me God, he was whistling some damned silly tune I'd heard the previous day on the Cortina's radio.

He began his approach against a tumbling

kaleidoscope of jagged crags and driving sleet. I could hear Innsbruck yelling at him, a constant crackle in the earphones clamped around his head. It was barely dusk, but up ahead, every light in the airport blazed through the filthy weather. Harvey seemed to be holding the 125 by an effort of naked will. We bucketed lower through the closing walls of the mountains, and I heard the triple *thunk* of the undercarriage locks. One long bounce on the runway threw up a hissing curtain of muck and slush. Then we thumped again, and Harvey held her down to stay. He turned as the brakes took hold, and flashed me his broken tooth.

'Hope you brought a change of underwear.'

I decided then that, too young or no, Sam Harvey would pass muster. He told me as we taxied back towards the control tower that he would arrange hangar space for the 125 at least until the weather cleared, and to get in touch with him at the airport when I was ready to make the return trip. The 125, with its range of nearly two thousand miles, had more than enough fuel for the flight back, and he could turn about at any time. Including now, if I felt up to it.

He let me out near Immigration, and I lugged my suitcase through the squalling rain into the welcome warmth. My passport aroused no undue excitement, although the Customs officer muttered something as I moved away about *verdammt blöde Engländer*. I found the driver, who had been alerted to stand by in spite of the airport's having been closed, in the little café-cum-duty-free shop. He left his coffee when I came in, and I let him. It was nearly ten to eight, we had a ninety-mile drive in front of us, and I was hungry. We went out at once and got into the Mercedes.

The driver was a squat, taciturn man with a belly on him like a Japanese wrestler. He slumped round-shouldered over the wheel peering past the swishing wipers in surly silence. When the madly swaying trailer towed by an enormous Italian lorry threatened on a bad steep bend to sweep us off the road he loosed a stream of language that would have made a docker blush. When I agreed with him, in German a little less lurid, he bared his stained dentures in an apologetic grin and spent the next ten minutes telling me just what a menace those *scheiss Italiener* bastards really were.

I sympathised, and asked him how long he'd had this job. Eleven years, nearly twelve. Then he would remember, I said, the accident in which a lady had lost her life. Oh yes, *Gott in Himmel*, he remembered that, all right. He took one hand off the wheel and crossed himself vigorously. He also eased off, I noticed, on the accelerator. But for an attack of food poisoning, there but for the Grace of God went he. The woman had come with Cooks, and since he was the driver regularly chartered by that splendid company he would, had he been fit, quite certainly have made the pick-up. He was, of course, a much better driver than the one who had killed both himself and his passenger, but it made a man stop and think all the same. He talked fast, but I got most of what he said and some of it was interesting.

Ilse Chisholm had been on the list of assignments given to him the previous evening by Fräulien Lovell, Cooks' permanent representative at the Hotel Tiefenbrunner. Ordinarily, he would most certainly have been at the airport next morning to pick her up. But something he had eaten at supper had disagreed with him, and he was bedridden for two whole days. Yes, he *had* known the substitute driver. He was an elderly fellow from the neighbouring village of Auwirt. Too old, really, for this run. Especially now, with these *verdammt Italiener* roaring along the road as though they owned it. He would not be surprised even if one of those *Schweine* had been responsible for the very accident about which we were talking...

I asked him to show me the place where it had happened. After about forty minutes, and one or two false stops, he pulled up just beyond a sharp bend on the side of a long hill. I got out, and walked back to the spot he had indicated as we crawled past. It was growing dark, but I could still see where part of the low stone retaining wall had been knocked down and rebuilt. I climbed over, and sank up to the ankles in thawing snow. The ground fell away from the road at a gradient of about one in eight. The timber had been cleared to a distance of thirty or forty yards, and the stumps stuck up like broken teeth. A car travelling at sufficient speed to smash through the wall would somersault off that lot like something out of a Steve McQueen movie.

I thought of scrambling down to the edge of the standing timber, but the fast-going light and the prospect of snow-soaked socks put me off. I might see some old scars and scorch marks where the car had fetched up, but there would not be anything more. I climbed back over the wall, and returned to the Mercedes. The driver was waiting resignedly, his engine still rumbling. He seemed to have exhausted his stock of conversation and, except for the times we were buffeted by the slipstream of a passing Italian truck, drove the rest of the way to Kitzbuhel in silence. We hit the town a little before ten. It was too dark for me to see much of it.

A patient *Kellnerin* was waiting in the Tiefenbrunner's big dining room to serve me, and I ate in solitary splendour. The food was reheated, and only fairly good, but it tasted marvellous. I boosted the delicious Viennese

68

coffee with a slug of cognac, tried one of their Austrian cigars, and went upstairs feeling very tired. My room on the third floor was at the end of the house, under the sharp slope of the eaves. I cleaned my teeth, opened the double windows to let in the mountain air—and crawled beneath the great downy quilt. Minutes later I was warm as toast, and drifting swiftly into the arms of Morpheus.

MONDAY

Next thing I knew, the room was filled with sunshine, and a plump and plaited picture-book Austrian lass was smiling down at me over a steaming coffee pot. It began to seem very pleasantly as though I really had started out on my spring week. I bathed and shaved and took about as long again to get all the plastic clips off one of the shirts I'd bought just a couple of days ago in York.

It was between seasons, and the dining room was less than half full. But I'd have spotted Miss Lovell in standing room only. She was sitting at a small table over against the wall, intent whilst eating on a thick Penguin propped against the coffee pot. I went over and stood with my hands on the back of the chair opposite.

'Miss Lovell?'

She looked up. Nice blue eyes, good features, short dark hair streaked handsomely with undisguised grey. Trim figure somewhat past its best, but held firmly in good posture. Hands a little too large, but still smooth and beautifully kept. Teeth, when she smiled, square and clean. My two typewritten pages had her down as age forty-six, resident in Kitzbuhel ten months of every year, her salary from Cooks supplemented by the usual representatives' tips and perks, and a small pension from a grateful nation. Her husband, a captain in the Engineers, had been killed in Burma towards the end of the war.

'Yes?'

'My name's Bill Thompson, and I'd like to talk to you. All right if I sit down?'

'Please do.'

Miss Lovell closed her book, and waved me into the chair facing her own. My beaming lass of the early morning brought more coffee, and the usual couple of rolls. I would rather have had sausage, eggs and bacon. Miss Lovell watched me spread jam, smiling ever so slightly as though she knew exactly what I was thinking. I liked her. I thought that, given a little time, she and I might very quickly become rather more than just good friends. I'd a distinct feeling that she was of the same opinion. It was that kind of meeting.

70

She remembered the accident quite well, and told me how sorry she had been for the young son who had come over to identify the body. Such a handsome lad, and so capable in what must have been a very harrowing experience. She'd helped him all she could, although his command of the language, and his competence at dealing with the Austrian officials, made her assistance hardly necessary. Fortunately, there had been plenty of insurance, so his expenses were practically nil. The whole sad business had been conducted with smooth efficiency. He had come to Kitzbuhel, made all the necessary arrangements, and departed with his mother's remains all in less than forty-eight hours.

'That's pretty fast work. What about police procedures? Wasn't there an inquest?'

'Oh, yes,' Miss Lovell smiled. 'But don't forget that it all happened at the height of the season, and that Kitzbuhel gets its living off the tourist trade. The town worthies just wanted to get the whole thing over and done with and quietly forgotten. The boy was willing to co-operate, so there was a minimum of fuss all round.'

'Do you remember the name of the undertaker?'

'Yes, it was old Johann Kurnich. His place is out towards the end of the town, near the sawmill . . .' Miss Lovell broke off, and her blue eyes quizzed me shrewdly. 'But what's all this about? Are you something to do with the family? It all happened so long ago . . .'

'No, no, I'm just an assessor. We're reshaping our standard contracts and this is simply, well, a kind of test case if you like. There's no dispute or anything, so you needn't worry about being hauled up as any sort of witness!' The way she laughed was a shared delight. I wondered if there might possibly be time. Then I remembered Charlie, and abandoned the idea. She asked if I would be going to see old Kurnich, and volunteered to come and show me the way. I told her I'd like that, but I'd other calls to make and would not wish to take up so much of her time. She said that was all right, but when I declined a second time sensibly refrained from pushing it. I asked her one more question.

'This chap who discovered the accident—do you know where I might find him, too?'

'Well, I know who he is. Young Gerhard Lukas. His people keep the little restaurant up on Kitzbuhel Horn. You reach it by the cable car . . .'

I thanked her. She stepped outside with me to point the way, and we fixed to meet up for lunch.

It has been said that Kitzbuhel is the prettiest town in the Tyrol. Whoever said it will get no argument from me. That morning, with the sun shining on the mountains all round, it was a travel agent's dream. The place was redolent of coffee and wine and cheerful cleanliness. I walked along the Franz-Erler-Strasse and came, as Miss Lovell had promised I would, to the sawmills. Johann Kurnick's funeral parlour was nice and handy. A small bell tinkled discreetly as I opened the door, and I stepped out of bright sunshine into cultivated gloom. A stout young man with a pale face and a dark suit appeared from behind a curtain and offered to do whatever he could for me. I asked if Herr Kurnick was around.

'*Jawohl. Er ist in der Werkstatt.*'

I told him it was very important, and that if I could just go through into the workshop I would not keep the *Leichenbestatter* more than just a few minutes. He hesitated, then nodded. I followed him through the curtain. The velvet-draped antechamber stank of old flowers and stale incense. A wreath-covered coffin stood on a couple of fancy trestles, watched over by a gilt-framed picture of a bearded man with his heart laid bare. I marvelled at the fire risk represented by the guttering candles.

The old man was at work on a new box. He turned as I came in, the heavy smoothing plane still cradled in his gnarled hands. Without his apron, and in a big spiked helmet, he would have been Hindenburg to the life. Close-cropped head, jutting nose, bushy white brows—the lot. His moustache was fierce

73

enough to intimidate an Irish navvy.

'Herr Kurnich?'

'Ja, ich bin Johann Kurnich. Was wollen Sie?'

I spun him my yarn, begged pardon for interrupting his work, and asked him if he could confirm my information that he had taken care of the accident victims. His nod was peremptory. He did not relinquish his hold on the plane. His manner said clearly that he wasn't about to waste a lot of time answering stupid questions.

'Ja, das ist ganz richtig.'

I tried to warm him up with a few routine queries, but it was like trying to thaw a glacier with a night-light. I asked him if he had been present at the identification. He grunted.

'Ja—natürlich. Der Junge, ihr Sohn, nahm den Leichnam mit nach England.'

I told him yes, I knew that the son had come for the body. Then I sprang a big one on him. I asked if the dead woman had been wearing any jewellery. His brows lowered.

'Nein, sie trug keinen Schmuck. Uberhaupt keinen.'

He seemed very sure about it. She was wearing no jewellery. None at all. I nodded, then feigned a further thought. 'Not even a wedding ring?'

'Bitte?'

He wasn't just begging my pardon. He was asking me just what the hell I meant by presuming to doubt his word. I asked him again, and he lost what was left of his temper.

'*Um Gottes Willen, ich hab's Ihnen schon gesagt! Sie trug nicht einmal einen Trauring—verstehen Sie? Und jetz, wenn Sie es erlauben, muss ich wieder an die Arbeit...*'

He turned his back on me and fetched a great curling swipe of wood off the edge of his coffin lid. End of interview. I thanked him for his ill-given time, and got out of there. I didn't want to excite him further by asking for a description of the dead woman. Charlie might not like it, but the fact that she wore no wedding ring would just have to be enough.

It was good to be out in the sunshine, and I stopped to wash away the taste of the funeral parlour with a cup of fragrant coffee. Then I walked out to the edge of town, and through the car park to the cable-railway station. I paid my fare, and climbed up to the car already waiting at the platform. It was a small one, a little four-seater. I got in, and sat there waiting for someone else to come along and make up the load. After a while the attendant got tired of waiting too. He came out of his chalet, locked the car door, and rang his bell for take-off. A couple of jerks, then the car climbed smooth as silk. The town fell away rapidly. Soon I was swaying in mid-air, high over the mountainside. The shrinking drifts on the lower slopes stood out white and crisp against the fresh green pasture.

I changed at the *Platzeralm* halfway station for the second stage of the lift. The car was a much bigger one with room for about forty standing passengers. Again I was the only occupant. The car swayed eerily through a couple of cloudbanks, then emerged at the snow-clad summit into bright sun. But it was very cold, and I was glad to get off the windswept platform and down into the restaurant.

It was just a tea-room, really. Beverages, soft drinks, and several revolving racks of picture postcards. The elderly Frau behind the counter had only three other clients, two women and a man. I got her to admit she was Frau Lukas, then asked where I might find her son. She told me he was here, fixing tiles on the lavatory wall, and went to get him. Whilst she was gone, I looked at some postcards and at my fellow customers.

The women were tourists, sitting together at a table by one of the windows and ooh-ing and aah-ing as they pointed out different aspects of the view. The man sat alone near the big square stove immersed, it seemed, in a copy of *Die Welt*. He was hunched inside a light overcoat, and had not taken off his hat. All I could see of him was a broad back. When the old lady returned, he motioned for her to bring him another cup of whatever it was he was drinking.

'Bitte—Sie wollten mich sehen?'

He was dark and thin, with an intelligent face. About twenty-three. He wiped some of the plaster off his hands down the front of overalls already well smeared with the stuff, and gave me a fistful of what was left.

'Gerhard Lukas?'

'Ja, ich bin Lukas. Was kann ich für Sie tun?'

I got us two cups of coffee, and sat down at a table near the counter. He seemed to believe my insurance assessor story, and said he was willing to help in any way he was able. I asked him to tell me everything he could remember. He said O.K.

There wasn't really very much to it. He and his father had been driving towards Innsbruck, to visit relatives there. They must have come upon the scene of the crash very soon after it happened. The car, badly smashed, was lying upside down against the trees. It was on fire, but he had managed to drag the old man—the driver—out of the wreckage without being burned himself. Boot lid and doors had burst open, and the lady had been thrown out. She was lying against a stump. The slope was littered with scattered luggage and bits of smoking Mercedes.

His father had driven on to the nearest telephone, and he himself had clambered down to see what he could do for the victims. Both were dead. Oh yes, they were dead, all right.

77

Must have been instantaneous. What a crash! It was terrible. Absolutely terrible. No, he had no idea what caused the accident. It was summer, and of course the road was quite clear and dry. Yes, well, he too had heard suggestions that the car had probably been side-swiped by one of the *verdammte Italiener*, but who could tell? Not the police, anyway. Their enquiries along those lines had got them nowhere. It was a mystery. *Verflucht rätselhaft.*

I asked him if there was anything about the crash which seemed strange to him. Anything at all. He thought for a while, then shook his head. But I seemed to detect some slight uncertainty. I pressed him again. He laughed self-consciously, drained his coffee, and studied the dregs. I waited.

'*Nun ...*' he began hesitantly, '... *da war etwas. Aber Sie werden mich wahrscheinlich für dumm halten...*'

I assured him I would not think him foolish. He shrugged, and went on.

As he was hauling the bodies further away from the burning wreckage he had noticed, as one sometimes does notice such trifles, that the woman had lost a shoe. He had looked for the other one as he gathered up the scattered luggage and assumed, when he could not find it, that it must be lost in the blaze...

So?

Well, this was the crazy part. So crazy that he

78

hadn't dared, afterwards, to tell anyone. He didn't know why, but the poor woman had looked curiously naked without her shoe. So, and don't ask what made him do it, he had tried to fit her with some he'd picked up. A pair flung out of the busted suitcase.

And?

'Die Schuhe passten ihr nicht, mein Herr. Sie waren zu klein. Sie waren viel zu klein!'

I went outside and sat in the waiting cable car. I wondered if, had Lukas told the police at the time that the woman's shoes were too small for her, it would have made any difference. Probably not. Young Chisholm had identified the body—and who was to suggest he could not possibly know his own mother? I looked at my watch. One o'clock. Back now to the Tiefenbrunner, lunch with the doomed-to-disappointment Miss Lovell, then back to Charlie with all the latest.

The cable-car man despaired eventually of my ever getting a fellow passenger, and came outside to lock me in for the descent. As he put his key in the door, there was a shout from the stairs. The man in the light overcoat came rushing up, thanked the attendant for holding the car, and set himself in the corner diagonally opposite mine. As we set off, he smiled.

'Wie schön ist es heute! Sie auf Urlaub hier in Kitzbuhel?'

His accent, not English, was worse than

mine. I pushed my belly against the waistband of my trousers, feeling in vain for the comforting bulge of the Smith & Wesson. No hardware, Charlie had said. Why hadn't I told him to go and bugger himself. The man reached inside his overcoat, and I braced myself for the jump. He came up with a gunmetal cigarette case.

I told him no, I was not on holiday. It was more of a business trip. I refused a cigarette, and watched him light his. I bunched my right hand inside my raincoat pocket. Some deterrent. We exchanged a few remarks about the beauties of the terrain. My mind raced.

We were locked in the car, and the station attendant had almost certainly signalled his chums below that there were two passengers. So what was there to worry about. I stepped across the car on the pretence of wanting to see something on that side, and stuck close to his elbow, ready to take him at the first sign of any move. The five minutes it took to drop down to the *Platzerlam* were the longest I'd ever spent.

I let him precede me, and we changed cars without incident. He had given up trying to make small talk, and we passed the second stage of the descent in strained silence. By the time we hit bottom I could feel the sweat running down the backs of my legs, and the muscles ached with tension. I kept behind him out of the station, and tailed him through the town.

He turned in at the Tiefenbrunner.

He lunched alone at a table across the room from ours, and I asked Miss Lovell if she knew him. She did.

'Oh, yes. That's Mr. Husak. He's been here since Sunday. He'll be going home tomorrow, like as not.'

Husak, it seemed, was a salesman for a small Czechoslovakian glass and chinaware outfit. Had been coming to Kitzbuhel twice a year for as long as Miss Lovell could remember. He would spend several days scouring the shops and restaurants for orders, then take himself off to his next port of call. Always acted the gentleman, kept himself to himself. Paid his bills promptly, and never made a nuisance.

As though sensing that we were talking about him, Husak looked across the room. He caught my glance, and lifted a hand in recognition. I returned his salute, and we exchanged smiles. It looked like I'd been reading too many spy stories.

Miss Lovell wanted me not to go. She pointed out my mistake in thinking I could get a flight out of Innsbruck. I told her I had the offer of a lift in a private aircraft. She painted a graphic picture of the dangers of flying out of that airport, and said she could book me on to a nice safe Trident leaving Munich tomorrow morning. I thanked her, said her offer was appreciated, but that if she really wanted to

81

help what about arranging a car for my trip back to the airport at Innsbruck. She wasn't happy, but went off to fix it. When she was gone, I telephoned the airport and got hold of the Customs officer. He promised to let Sam Harvey know that I'd be back, ready for take-off, at about 1630.

Miss Lovell had been patently upset to see me hurry through the excellent lunch she had ordered for us, but cheered up again when I told her I liked Kitzbuhel very much and thought I'd come back later in the year for a holiday. She said she'd still be here, and would look forward to it. I should let her know when it was to be, and she would use her influence to get me a good room. I said I certainly would. At the time, I meant it. She dropped a charming hint that she was free for the rest of the day, and would not mind coming to the airport with me, just for the ride. I let it pass.

We parted outside of the Tiefenbrunner, and I spent the first half-hour of the drive out in pleasant speculation of my return to Kitzbuhel, and renewed acquaintance with the fair Enid. That was her name—Enid. My reveries were rudely interrupted. We rounded a long curve, and I was thrown forward in my seat as the driver slammed on his brakes. We got out.

A heavy lorry with a high load of planks and battens had taken the bend too sharply. It lay on its side, completely blocking the road. There was timber everywhere. The *Polizei* were on the scene already. One of them was kneeling beside the driver of the lorry, who was lying on the bank. The other officer was leaning in at the open window of the police car talking into a hand mike. I left it to my driver to go up and ask what the score was. He came back to the car shaking his head.

It was not bad, just awkward. The lorry driver was shocked and shaken, but had no broken bones. *Die Polizei* had radioed for the ambulance and a mobile crane, but the latter might take an hour to get here. No, there was no way round. We'd just have to hang about until the road was cleared. He climbed into the front passenger seat and settled back philosophically to wait. I told him I would walk on ahead to the next roadside telephone box, and to look for me there when he was able to follow on with the car. He shrugged O.K.

Any other time, the walk would have been invigorating. It was a fine day, with just enough nip in the air to make walking quite pleasant. Sun and snow and mountain air, and a refreshing fragrance off the pines. But I was worried about the delay, and anxious to let Sam Harvey know what was going on. I covered the six or seven miles into Worgl with unnecessary haste and, after a series of false starts and frustrating delays, finally got Harvey on the other end of the telephone line.

'Sam? This is Farrow. Yes, I know. Look, there's a hold-up. No, no ... just an accident on the road...'

I told him what had happened and that no, I didn't think any of it had been contrived. I agreed it was *possible*. He suggested I get another car in Worgl. I said I would try, but that I thought my own must be along very soon now, anyway. I did not tell him that I'd been stupid enough to leave my suitcase behind. He said all right then, he'd get back to the kite and just wait for me to show up. He'd slept in the 125, and did not like to leave it unattended for too long. I did a little mental sum and told him that I hoped, all being well, to see him now around 1800. Six o'clock.

But it was closer to seven when I got to the airport, and some time afterwards before we finally took off. The Customs lad appeared to take longer with my meagre luggage than he really need have done. I thought at one stage he was going to ask me to strip. Sam Harvey seemed somehow to have aged at least five years, and he trundled the Hawker Siddeley up to the end of the runway in curious silence. He pulled the 125 into a steep full-throttles take-off with none of his usual cheeky repartee. I sat beside him in the cockpit, listening to the crackle from the spare headset slung over the co-pilot's control column. Sam remained uncommunicative, and I moved back later into

84

the cabin to stretch out in one of the seats. I dozed off.

I was awakened by Sam nudging at my shoulder. He appeared to have regained his old humour.

'Wake up, you lazy sod, and fasten your belt. We're over old Albion, and I'll be putting her down in about five minutes. Here'—he thrust a scrap of paper into my hand—'you're to ring that number when you've cleared the airport. Usual procedure. If McGowan doesn't answer, ring it again at intervals of twenty minutes. O.K.?'

Harvey put the little aeroplane down on to the dark airfield light as a feather, and we taxied over towards the lights of the airport buildings. It was twenty past nine. I shook hands with Harvey, and thanked him. He said nothing to it, boy. Any time. Any time at all. The elderly officer in the tiny Customs shed just looked quickly at my passport and told me there was a mini cab waiting. More of Harvey's work. I asked the driver to hang on, got to a phone, and dialled the number. I let it ring at the other end the usual dozen times, then three more for good measure. No reply. I got into the mini cab and told the driver to head for Huddersfield.

I stopped him at a call box on the Bradford ring road, and tried again to get Charlie. This time, he answered.

'Farrow? What gives?'

I started to tell him first about the hold-up, but he cut me short.

'Yes, yes—I got all that. Harvey's radio message was passed on to me. What about the Chisholm thing?'

I told him quickly all that had happened, and what I thought about it. He was silent for several seconds. Then:

'There is some corner of a Huddersfield cemetery . . .'

'. . . that is for ever foreign field,' I said. 'Yes, I'd say that's about the size of it. What now?'

'Young Chisholm's done a bunk. That's what now.'

'*What?*'

'You heard me. I had a local man on him. He left his lodgings at half past seven to drive down to work. He's got the graveyard shift this week—eight o'clock till four in the morning. The local man tailed him down to Fylingdales, saw him into the tunnel, then reported to me that he'd arrived. What he didn't report, because he didn't know, was that Chisholm drove into the station, straight through the place, and out again by the tunnel on the far side. By the time anybody with any sense knew anything about it, the little bastard had disappeared.'

'So what do we do?'

'I just came back here to wait for your next call. I'm going down now to Fylingdales. I don't suppose there'll be any lead there, but if there is I shall be following up. You go back to Huddersfield and wait for word from Jock.'

'Does Jock know about Chisholm yet?'

'No. We've had no contact since teatime. He was supposed to call in at nine. I think he must be on to something. Anyway, no use you running around like a chicken with its head cut off. Just get back to the George and wait for one of us to get in touch. All right?'

I said all right, and got back into the cab in the grip of an uncomfortable feeling that events were running away from us. I hadn't told Charlie about Husak, and wondered now if I should have. Perhaps my premonitions in the cable car had not been so foolish after all. I thought about it, and began to put a new interpretation on Husak's smile at lunchtime. This reminded me that it had been eight hours and nearly a thousand miles since my last meal. The thought made me hungry. I stopped the cab at a fish and chip shop I knew in Oakenshaw. Three pieces of fish and five new pence-worth of chips, plenty of salt and vinegar. I ate them on the way back. Marvellous. Fit for a king.

We got to the George, what with the stops and all, just before eleven. I paid off the driver and—what the hell, it wasn't my money—delighted him with a 50p tip. The old lad on night porter duty told me that a chap in a soft hat had been in looking for me. Around about half-nine. No, he hadn't left a note or anything, he'd just said to tell me that Mr. Harris had been, and would call again later.

I got the old lad to serve me with a pint in the residents' lounge, and filled a pipe. Later, I had another pint, and another pipe. At midnight I was the only one left in the lounge, and the old man was fussing around with the ashtrays. He managed to make me aware that I was sitting in his favourite chair. I left him a couple of new 10p bits, asked him to wake me if there was a call of any kind, and went upstairs to bed.

TUESDAY

The old porter woke me in the morning at ten to seven, forty minutes before I'd told him to. He was bent over the bed to shake my shoulder, his face a foot from mine. He looked scared. When I'd got my eyes properly opened, I saw why. At his back was an enormous copper and beyond him, at the open door, stood another. I sat up.

'Hello? What's all this, then?'

'Mr. Farrow? M. A. Farrow?'

'That's right. What can I do for you?'

The old man ducked out from under and edged, crabwise, away. The bobby nearest the bed stepped back a pace, and the one in the doorway moved over solidly to block the exit. And me stark naked, defenceless as a baby. I got my mind started, and up into second gear.

'Well, what's it all about?'

'Will you get dressed, sir, please.'

I got up and went to the washbasin. They watched me at my ablutions, and as I put on my clothes. When I was ready they stepped aside and let me precede them down the stairs. Waiting in the empty lounge was a uniformed inspector. He touched the peak of his cap with his swagger-stick.

'Good morning, sir. Mr. Farrow?'

I admitted it one more time. The two coppers lined themselves at my back, and the inspector looked me over. He seemed to be waiting for me to say something. I said it.

'Look, just what the hell do you people want?'

The inspector looked grave. He nodded at something or someone behind me, and one of his men told the old night porter that that would be all.

'Are you the M. A. Farrow who hired a blue Cortina, registration number BDN 735J from a garage in York on Saturday last?'

'I am. What about it?'

The inspector nodded, as though he'd known it all along. 'All in good time, sir. Would you mind coming along with us? We have a car outside.'

They herded me into the back seat of a black Jaguar. With one of the big peelers on either side, it was a tight squeeze. His nibs climbed in beside the driver. We drew away from the front of the hotel, rounded the bottom of the railway station, and shot across the near-deserted town centre to run up past the infirmary and out on to Trinity Hill. Then the driver opened up, and we did the long straight mile of New Hey Road in under a minute. Almost before I knew it, we were up on Outlane Moor and braking hard to turn into a narrow cart track. The Jag bumped slowly down the rough dirt lane, with barely enough room between the broken stone walls for the car to pass. Then we came up against the Jag's twin sister, and were forced to stop. When I got out I could see, beyond the second police car, the blue Cortina. Both front doors were flung wide open. Someone or something was lying in a heap beneath the open door on the driver's side, and it was lying very still.

One of the men already there was a uniformed sergeant. The other two were in civvies. Him on my side of the car tried to stop me. I pushed him hard and he fell against the stone wall. I hope he hurt his back. I dropped down on to my knees in the wet muck. The man I'd pushed scrambled up, and grabbed himself a fistful of my collar. I told him, not looking round, to get his hand off. I knew without seeing him that he glanced across at the inspector. The inspector told him to get his hand off. I bent my head and closed my eyes and when I opened them again I was still looking at Jock.

He was lying face down alongside of the car, right arm stretched straight out in front. His grip on the Smith & Wesson had not relaxed. His left arm was bent sharply under him, the hand clutching at something small which was sticking out of his neck. There was a lot of blood. It was splashed all over the dash, and down the inside of the door. He was lying in a pool of the stuff. Whoever had killed him knew exactly where the jugular was.

I don't know how long I knelt there. It was probably not more than a few seconds. When I stood up, they were all looking at me. I took the inspector's arm and drew him away beyond the cars. He glanced down at my etching, and nodded.

'Yes, I thought so. We found one like it on your friend. What's up?'

Thank God for a sensible one. I told him I needed to make a contact, and asked him to be sure in the meantime that nothing here was moved or disturbed. Also to keep tight wraps on it. He gave the necessary orders and came back with me to town. One of the plain-clothes men, not the one I'd shoved, came along too and got out of the car with me at the hotel. I left him downstairs in the lounge and went up to my room.

My own Smith & Wesson was still there where I'd hidden it before going off to Kitzbuhel. I got it out, dusted it off, and checked the cylinder. All present and correct. I stuck the gun back in its little holster and clipped it firm to the inside of my waistband. There was no telephone in my room, so I went back down to the booth in the lobby. I didn't really expect Charlie to be at yesterday's number and he wasn't. But he rang in just as I was about to break into my second egg. I got to the phone and told him why Jock had failed last night to make contact. He was silent for so long I thought he must have hung up.

'Charlie?'

'Yes, I'm still here.' He sounded tired. 'Look, I'm near Fylingdales. They've got a helicopter there, and I'm going to borrow it. I'll meet you at the ... at the ... where it happened, in an hour. Yes ... I've got it ... about two miles east north-east of town. We'll find you. Yes. Listen—tell the bobbies we want it kept quiet. Oh, you already did, did you. Good. Right then, see you soon.'

Back at the breakfast table, I took the top off my second egg, then found I didn't want it. I hadn't wanted the first one. The plain-clothes man sensibly refrained from trying to make talk. Huddersfield water makes very good tea, and we emptied the pot in silence. I asked him if he could organise a car to take us back to Outlane Moor, and he went off to phone the station. It took them only about three minutes.

I heard the whopping of the helicopter's rotors and looked up to see it sweeping in on us with that curious sideways attitude. It swung down very fast, seemed somehow to brake, and hung over us swaying gently whilst the pilot picked his place. He chose a spot not thirty yards away. I stood there with my hands in my raincoat pockets and watched the thing squat down on to the moorland turf like an old hen settling on a clutch of chicks. Charlie jumped out, waved the pilot noisily up and away again, and turned towards us. He just nodded, squeezed past me in the lane and knelt, as I had done, beside old Jock.

A small noise escaped him, and I moved away. I didn't want to look. I was afraid I might see something for which Charlie would never forgive me. So I picked my way over stones tumbled from the old wall, and said something meaningless to the plain-clothes man. The one I'd pushed. Our spell of forced chit-chat was soon interrupted.

'Farrow ...' Charlie was his old self, only more so. He had taken up Jock's gun, and none of your pencil-down-the-barrel stuff. He was hefting the pistol in his hand. '... it looks like Jock got one away. If he did, my money says he hit something . . .'

How I hoped he was right. A slug from a Smith & Wesson .357 magnum has a muzzle velocity of nearly 1500 feet per second, and a muzzle energy of around 700 foot pounds. With that much gun you need very little more than a near miss. Hit a man *anywhere*, and he goes down. Do anything more than just clip him, and he stays down.

'I hope he hit something,' I said. 'I hope to Jesus he did.'

'Yes, well'—his eyes behind the rimless specs were calm now, and expressionless—'we'll need to find out, won't we?'

The Huddersfield law could not have been more helpful. They looked after Jock's body and, after we'd gone over the Cortina with a fine-tooth comb, cleaned it up like new. They gave us a room at the police station, and made us a pot of coffee. We sat at a little wooden table on top of which was spread the stuff from Jock's pockets. Charlie was examining the sliver of steel which the police surgeon had taken out of Jock's neck.

It was a lovely piece of stuff, all right. About six inches long and not much more than a quarter of an inch wide. No thicker anywhere than a hacksaw blade. The last two inches were honed at both edges, literally razor-sharp. Whoever it belonged to had probably carried it concealed in the lapel of his coat. Charlie flicked his fingers and the little knife turned over out of his hand and stuck quivering in the table top. Right next to the aspirin bottle.

'You better get down there.'

'Down where?'

'The chemist's, of course.' Charlie picked up the little bottle and read the tiny print at the bottom of the label. 'B. T. Hinchcliffe, 73 Newport Street, Huddersfield.'

'I don't get it.'

'Ask yourself.' Charlie unscrewed the bottle cap and began to draw out the wad of cotton-wool packing. It was stuffed in tight, and the bottle was full. He shook out the pills, and counted them off into five lots of five. They were all there. 'What would Jock be doing with a bottle of aspirin?'

'Maybe he got a headache?'

'Jock Harris never had a headache in his life.'

'There's always a first time...'

I knew as soon as I'd got it out that it was the wrong thing to say. A strange man, Charlie. He just looked across the table at me, and pushed away his coffee cup. End of discussion. I stood up, and shrugged into my raincoat.

'Right then. Where are you going to be?'

'Here, I suppose ... Yes, come back here.' Charlie poked with his clean scrubbed finger at the pathetic assortment of Jock's effects. Wallet, diary, half a roll of Polo mints, hard money, pen, wrist watch, cheque book and hankie. 'Simmonds'—that was the inspector, gone home now for his breakfast—'has put a detail on old Ma Chisholm's place. Our man isn't likely to try it, but if he does, we'll know. Meantime, I've got a report to make. So see why the aspirin bit, and we'll go on from there.'

I took the Cortina. Newport Street was a little way out of the town centre, a turning off the main road to Manchester. The shop was an old one, its faded façade made to look even drabber by the new plastic front of the TV shop next door. The fly-flecked display packs in the window were all out of date. Yesterday's products in a world of constant tomorrow. Inside, more of the same. The walls were lined all the way round from floor to ceiling with glass-fronted cabinets packed with pills, potions, and aids to instant beauty. The girl behind the old-fashioned mahogany counter, though, was bright and cheerful and seemed intelligent. 'Is Mr. Hinchcliffe about, please?'

She laughed and shook her head. 'No. Mr. Jowett, you mean. I think old Mr. Hinchcliffe must be dead by now. Mr. Jowett took over, like, when Mr. Hinchcliffe retired—oh, it must be ten year back. Before I started here, anyway. Didn't you know?'

'No,' I said. 'Well, I'll see Mr. Jowett, then.'

'Do you know,' she looked up at the ceiling as she spoke, 'I don't think he's in. If he is, he must be still asleep. I haven't heard him moving

96

about. But he's usually down long before this time. It's a wonder I had the key with me...'

I looked at my watch. Twenty minutes past ten. Something was happening to the hairs at the back of my neck. 'Look, love,' I said, 'it's important. Could you just nip up and see if he's there?'

She hesitated, then nodded. 'All right, then. I won't be a minute.'

She went through a door at the rear of the shop and I caught a glimpse of carpeted stairs leading up to the apartment above. True to her word she was back, frowning, in about one minute flat.

'That's funny, he must have gone off somewhere. Except I don't think he's been in—unless he made his bed and everything before he went out. But he's never done it before. Not without telling me. In't that peculiar?'

I said that it was, and let her see the aspirin bottle. 'This one of yours?'

She took the bottle from my hand and read the label. 'Oh, yes, that's one of ours. Where did you get it?'

I told her I'd got it from the chap who had bought it here yesterday, and she shook her head. She shook it very firmly.

'No, it wouldn't have been yesterday, mister. He didn't buy it yesterday. Mr. Jowett was away, and I was here all day by myself. I didn't sell any twenty-five bottle of BP yesterday.'

'Are you sure?'

'Oh, yes,' she nodded forcefully. 'I'm positive. We don't sell a lot of BP, you know. Most folk'd rather pay five times as much for t'same thing in a fancy packet. I haven't sold a bottle of BP since ... oh ... one day last week.'

'So you're sure,' I insisted, 'that this bottle of aspirin wasn't bought in this shop yesterday?'

She nodded again. 'Yes, I've told you. I'm quite sure—oh!' She broke off abruptly and clapped a hand over her mouth. I waited for it. 'Just a minute, though! Last night was our turn for prescriptions. Yes, I clean forgot about that! I never do prescription night, Mr. Jowett always does it hisself. I finish at six o'clock, you see...'

She was talking about the system by which local chemists arrange for one of their number to remain open until seven-thirty or eight in order to fill prescriptions written by doctors at evening surgery. They usually take it in turn. This put Jock here in the shop between six and eight o'clock last night. When they found him up on Outlane Moor at five-thirty in the morning he had been dead, they reckoned, for six to nine hours. I suddenly wanted very badly to see Mr. Jowett.

'I wonder where he can be,' I said.

The girl shrugged. 'I'm sorry, I just haven't a clue. I don't know anywhere he went—apart from that club of theirs down on Wakefield Road. But he wouldn't be there at this time on a morning, would he now?'

Something moved in the bottom of my gut. 'At the Polish Club, d'you mean? No, I don't suppose he'd be there . . .'

'Here, just a minute'—I'd been right, this girl was no slouch—'I thought you said you didn't know Mr. Jowett?'

'No, I don't. But I know Wakefield Road. That Polish place is the only club along there, so far as I know. He's a Pole then, is he?'

'Oh, yes. He's nice, though—excuse me . . .'

The shop doorbell had jangled and she turned away from me to serve a woman in a head-scarf and curlers. Before this one had made up her mind over the merits of various cheap cough cures, someone else had come in. I made signs to the girl that I'd return later, and left.

Back at the police station, Inspector Simmonds told us what he knew about the Poles of Huddersfield. It turned out that there was a fair-sized community. Well on, now, into the second generation. Most of the original lot had been ex-army blokes who had stayed on after the end of the war. The Polish-Huddersfield stock were, of course, fully integrated, some of them with children of their own. Typically, though, the older ones clung together. They had their own club, their own

99

church—also on Wakefield Road—and most of them even attended the same doctor. A fellow Pole, of course, an elderly M.D. with a practice somewhere in the Almondbury area on the outskirts of town. Charlie asked Simmonds for the address, and we went out there together.

It was an old detached house with a bit built on at the end to serve as a surgery. The old woman who opened the door told us that she was the housekeeper, and the doctor was away on his rounds. We asked her how long she thought he would be. As she was trying to make up her mind, a car pulled in at the gate. Ah, she said, this was the doctor now. We let him get out of the car and told him what we wanted. He asked us in.

Dr. Bazcyk said he knew Jowett—Tadaeus Jowysz, actually—quite well. Naturally. He knew all of the Huddersfield Poles. Most of them had fought together in the same unit, and had formed the community here when they had been demobbed after the war. Not that he saw very much of Tadaeus these days, mind. He never was an ailing man, had not sought the doctor's professional services for a good number of years. Nor was he a regular church-goer, and this was unusual. Yes, he did go occasionally to the Polish Club on Wakefield Road, but even there he hadn't of recent years been inclined to mix much. He had in fact become more and more withdrawn. One might almost say of his

100

behaviour that it verged on the eccentric. Yes, he did have folks back in the old country. Some said a wife and children, but he, the doctor, did not know about that.

Bazcyk was an old man, certainly over seventy. He had a very courteous and gentle manner, and I got the impression that his education had fitted him for bigger things than the job of glorified prescription clerk. But he seemed happy in his work, and I was willing to bet that the patients on his panel were given treatment and advice far superior to that which most of them deserved or appreciated. I wondered what he thought about wasting his training on the cosseted scroungers of our Welfare State.

Charlie thought the old man clean, and so did I. We cut across Almondbury Bank on to Wakefield Road, and cruised along until we spotted the church. It stood in a neat little plot opposite a supermarket, a biggish corrugated-iron building painted all over a dull red. A crested board at the gate told everyone exactly what it was and, as though to remove any lingering doubt, the front of the pointed gable was decorated with a neon sign in the form of a cross. We drove on past and turned first left to park in a side road. As we were walking back, it began to rain.

The front entrance opened on to a short passage, with a door on each side. Both were closed. We went straight forward, and into the church proper. The interior, which was deserted, came as a big surprise. The Poles of Huddersfield were either very rich or they spent most of what they had on trappings for their way of worship. The far gable, not visible from the road, was composed almost entirely of stained glass, and the whole of the interior cladding was decorated with lavish art. Unless I was very much mistaken, the knick-knacks on and around the altar were made of the real McCoy. The statue of a lady with an infant chewing at her left teat had a wired-on halo which looked, even on that dull day, to be composed of liquid light. We stood there between the rows of carven pews and gazed at it all. Behind us, somebody coughed.

His accent and attitudes were Irish and proud of it. He took us into one of the little ante-rooms off the front—and only—entrance. A roll-top desk, a good steel safe, three hard chairs, and a nice thick carpet to keep the draught out. Looking down from the wall above the desk, a hideous wood and ivory artifact at least one quarter life-size. He sat at the desk, in the only decent chair, and put the tips of his fingers together. He favoured Charlie with a sweet sad smile.

'Mr. Jowett? No, my son'—he must have been all of twenty-eight years old—'I'm afraid Mr. Jowett is not as regular a communicant as you've been led to believe. Indeed, no'—even his melancholy chuckle smacked of auld Ireland—'although he means well, of course...'

'Of course.' Charlie kept his eyes on his hands, which hung limply between his knees. 'But tell me, Father, has he been to church—have you seen him recently at all?'

The priest did not even have to think. 'Not this year, no,' he said. 'We haven't seen him since Christmas. Not since the midnight Mass on Christmas Eve.' He seemed suddenly to realise that we were questioning him, and frowned. We were trespassing on his territory, ground that was sacrosanct. He remembered the nature of his authority. His quizzical stare switched from Charlie to me and back again to Charlie. 'But what in all the world is this about? Is Mr. Jowett in some kind of trouble?'

'Oh, no, no.' Charlie stood up, so I did too. 'Not that we know of. But he seems to have disappeared, and we're trying to trace him. Anyway, thanks for your help...'

The priest got up also, and raised the first three fingers of his right hand. I thought for a moment that he was going to send us on our way rejoicing. It was just, however, that we'd roused his curiosity. He wanted to know much more about what the hell was going on, and required us to tell him. He had about as much chance of intimidating Charlie as I had of

103

getting the Pope to canonise Luther. We took firm leave of him. Outside, the sky was dark, and the rain was coming down as though this was its last chance. We sprinted back to the car, tumbled in, and used our handkerchiefs to wipe off the worst of it. As I drew away from the kerb, Charlie looked at his watch.

'What about some lunch?'

I could have hugged him. I made a three-point turn, got back on to the main drag, then turned right into Kilner Bank. We came out on the Leeds Road, and I swung into the big car park at the Three Nuns. An army is only as good as the belly it marches on. Charlie looked up at the front of the place and scowled. I knew him well enough by now to know that he cared about expenses as though it were his own money. I turned off the engine, and buttoned up the collar of my raincoat prior to getting out. Charlie looked at his watch again. Wondering, no doubt, if it was too late to go and look for somewhere else.

'Don't worry about it, Charlie,' I said. 'If it comes too fierce, I'll pay for it myself.'

He shot me one of his empty looks, and ducked out. I watched him run for the steps through the teeming rain, wondering if I'd gone a bit too far. When I got in, though, he was almost amiable. He even bought me a pint. So I stuck to the *table d'hôte*, and kept it modest. Not that it would have mattered very much. It all went on my slop-chit, anyway. When the coffee came, we opted to have it in the deserted lounge bar. Charlie chose a table in the corner. He looked at my pipe as though it alone was responsible for polluting the environment.

'Do you have to smoke that thing?'

'No,' I said, 'I don't *have* to. But it's going to take more than the odd complaint to persuade me to stop it. So what shall we talk about now?'

'Jowett. You start. Let's have your thinking on the subject.'

So I told him what I thought. That Jock had got on to Jowysz, or Jowett, probably through the Polish Club lead we'd gleaned from old Ma Chisholm. That he'd gone along to the shop, found it open, and looked the place over on the pretext of buying aspirin. Less than twelve hours later he was dead, and Jowett had vanished. Events which were almost certainly connected. Ergo, find Jowett and get him to 'assist us in our enquiries'.

'Brilliant.' Charlie nodded. 'Bloody marvellous—but how?'

'How what?'

'How do we find Jowett?'

'I don't know. I thought *you* knew.'

And Charlie by God *did* know. He talked first with Inspector Simmonds, who sent a C.I.D. man to see the manager of the supermarket. By quarter to six, fifteen minutes after closing, we were sitting in front of the window in the staff-room up on the first floor, watching the rain come down. Our view of the church across the way was clear and unhampered. We had two flasks of tea and a packet of ham sandwiches to last us until the church closed its doors at eight o'clock. We were sitting in tubular-metal chairs with padded arm-rests, on either side of a plastic-topped table. Charlie was staring out into the rain and talking as though to himself.

'Please let Jock have hit him. Let him be running scared. Let the bugger be in terror of his mortal soul. Let him come ... let him come ... let him *come* ...'

I looked across at Charlie and wondered if it were possible for anyone really to like him. Probably not. A right dedicated bastard, he had the sort of iron discipline which reminds one all the time of one's own inadequacies. Not a big man, more of a pocket battleship. Compact and deadly and very, very dangerous. Even just sitting there quietly he was a bundle of smouldering force. Neat, even fastidious, a non-smoker and a non-drinker. A man of singular purpose, serenely aware of his identity and of his exact place in the overall scheme of things.

Most people would put his age at around the early thirties but with a man like Charlie it was difficult to tell. He could be into his forties, same as me. He leaned forward now to peer through the rivulets streaming down the window. Two people, a woman and child, were hurrying through the downpour towards the church. They scurried right past, and Charlie sat back. Apart from the drumming of rain on the roof, and the occasional swish of passing traffic, it was very quiet. I poured us each a flask-top full of tea.

'What are your hobbies, Chas?'

'Hobbies?' He never took his eyes off the church. 'What d'you mean, hobbies?'

'I mean what do you do when you're not working?'

'I'm never not working. Only time I'm not *consciously* working is when I'm asleep.'

I looked up from my tea and actually felt the smile die on my lips. He meant it. He quite simply and sure as hell meant every word of it. I didn't know what to say, so said nothing. Neither did he. After a while he took out a packet of paper hankies and got to work on his nose.

I began before our watch was half over to long for tobacco. Rain fell out of the darkening sky in a monotonous perpetual torrent. At the church, business was terrible. Only five people in the first hour, and not one of them even remotely like the one we were after. Charlie had sent for a mug shot and description of Jowett, and we knew exactly what we were looking for. At seven-thirty the street lights came on. I don't think Charlie had taken his eyes off the church once. I drank the rest of my flask of tea, ate the last of the sandwiches, and thought about Sarah Wade.

'Hey, Charlie...'

'What now?'

'You ever thought about getting married?'

Charlie brushed carefully at his clothes, just in case he'd made any crumbs, and screwed the top back on his empty flask.

'Don't be stupid.'

'What's stupid about it?'

He took his eyes off the church just long enough to give me one of his blank stares. He sighed, and turned back to the window.

'You got any sisters, Farrow?'

'Yes, I've got a sister. Why?'

Charlie smoothed the thin sandy hair along the side of his head. 'You fond of her?'

'Of course I am,' I said. 'Naturally.'

'Would you like to see her married to someone in our line of business?'

'Well ...' I remembered old Jock, lying in the mud beside the car.

'Right, then. Like I said. Don't be so damned stupid.'

It was beginning now to get really dark, and the rain had abated not one little bit. When I looked yet again at my watch it was almost eight o'clock. I started to gather up our gear, and the crumpled sandwich wrappers.

'Come on, Charlie. Let's bugger off. He's not going to come now.'

'Wait . . .'

A solitary figure had turned into the main road and was moving along the pavement in the direction of the church. It passed under a street-lamp, and we saw that it was a woman. We could tell she was elderly by the slow way she walked, and the length of her clothes. She was bundled up in a plastic mac with a cowl-like hood, and crouched under a man's black umbrella. Just as she turned in at the gate, the church's main lights snapped out. She collapsed the umbrella, hurried in at the door, and the lights went on again. I struggled into my damp raincoat, stuck a vacuum flask into each side pocket, and pulled my chair back away from the window.

'You ready, Chas?'

'All right, then.' Charlie sat tight. 'Go out the back way and bring the car along. I'll come when you've got it out front.'

That's what I'd thought. The privilege of command. I groped my way down the pitch-black stairs and let myself out of the back door. The alley alongside the store was unpaved, and I stepped into a puddle over the shoe tops. I crossed the road, turned right, made my squelching way to the side turning where we'd stashed the Cortina. By the time I was inside, the rain had flattened my hair and was running down my face. Then the engine didn't want to start. I finally got the damn thing to fire, and raced the motor to heat up the system and dry off the plugs. Charlie probably thought I'd got lost.

When I drew in at the kerb by the supermarket the woman was leaving the church. All of the lights were out now, and the priest had come out with her. They reached the gate just as I set the handbrake. The woman looked across at the car, said something to the priest, and turned away. There was a sudden crash from overhead, and I looked up to see that Charlie had flung open his window. He was yelling like crazy as I scrambled out, and the woman started to run.

'Farrow—get after her!'

She dropped her umbrella and picked up her skirts. I dashed headlong into the road, dragging at the Smith & Wesson. A motor horn screamed loud in my left ear, and a shower of spray from the car which swerved violently to miss me drenched my trouser legs. I made the opposite pavement, pushed past the gaping priest, and got into my stride. The woman had over a hundred yards on me, but was clutching at her side now and faltering badly. Then she reached the intersection. A car without lights jumped out of the side turning and jolted to a stop at the corner with its nearside door flying wide open.

I skidded to a halt and raised the Smith & Wesson at arm's length, both hands around the butt. The woman was lunging for the car, bent double to throw herself in. I blinked rapidly against the driving rain, thumbed back the hammer, and squeezed off. The pistol slammed against my palms, and the blast seemed to clatter all around the houses. The woman threw up her arms and the car took off with an agonised screeching of tyres. She was dragged crazily halfway into the main road, then flung sprawling on to the wet tarmac. I ran towards her, the vacuum flasks in my coat pockets bouncing clumsily against my pumping thighs.

The hood had fallen away from the woman's face and head. She had close-cropped grey hair, and a two-day stubble. I put the gun away, got him under the armpits, and dragged him back on to the pavement. Fortunately, there was no more traffic, and no one seemed disturbed by the shot. Jowett, or Jowysz, least of all.

'Is he dead?'

I looked up and nodded. Charlie swore.

'Bloody brilliant!'

I got to my feet, angry. 'Jesus Christ, Charlie—I *did* try to wing him! But bloody hell, man, it's dark and it's pissing down and he was sixty yards away. What was I supposed to do—let him break clear?'

'Never mind. Let's get him inside.'

We hauled him back into the church, and

Charlie made the priest lock the doors. The Irishman kept on gibbering about police and ambulance. Charlie told him to shut up. He was trembling, very badly scared. We laid the body down in the lobby and opened up his clothing. My slug had gone in at the back, and clipped the heart. It had made a big hole on its way out, and had probably missed getting the driver as well by not very much.

But he had another wound. In his side, and roughly dressed. A bad place to get hit, and it must have hurt like hell. Enough, anyway, to set him sweating with thoughts of the life hereafter. Charlie straightened up from looking at it, and pushed the priest into his little office.

'Get in there, Paddy. You and me've got things to talk about.'

I tagged in behind them and shut the door. I knew, of course, what Charlie was after. He had to know for sure if Jowysz had killed old Jock. I started to recall correct procedures for the questioning by two operatives of a hostile suspect. Charlie started right in. He shoved the cleric down into his own chair and leaned down over him with a hand on each of the chair arms.

'All right, priest-man,' he said softly. 'Just what was it that your friend Jowysz wanted to get off his chest?'

The priest looked up into Charlie's face, and I thought for a moment it was going to be that easy. Then he remembered who and where he was, and seemed to draw strength from every one of those two thousand infallible years. He shook his head.

'The Confession is inviolable...'

'Oh, we won't violate it much,' said Charlie. 'You just tell me, and I won't tell anybody else. How about that?'

The priest gained confidence. He went on shaking his head, and now even smiled. He thought he was dealing with a reasonable man. Poor sad bastard. Charlie sighed. He reached under his arm and let the priest take a look at the Smith & Wesson.

'You know what this is?' He chucked the cleric under the chin, quite gently at first, with the snub barrel. Then he put some pressure on, and held it. The poor man squinted down at the ugly gun, unable now to shake his head at all. Charlie lifted the pistol up and hooked the blunt foresight under his upper lip. He ground the muzzle against the priest's buck teeth. 'It's a martyr-maker, buddy,' he said softly. 'A thing used by people like me for making martyrs out of people like you. Now—what's your name?'

The priest strove to speak, and managed a dry sob. Charlie nudged his teeth again. He swallowed. 'O'Halloran,' he croaked. 'Father O'Halloran. I...'

Charlie rapped his teeth with the gun muzzle, this time harder. 'And you can cut out the "father" bit,' he said harshly. 'For all I know,

113

you might be a daddy a dozen times over, but you're certainly not mine. So just stuff all that kind of manure and talk plain English. You know what I mean?'

The priest nodded dumbly, too frightened now to speak at all. Charlie smiled. 'Right, then. Now—what's your name?'

'P ... P ... Patrick O'Hallor ...'

Charlie twitched the muzzle, and I saw blood flow as the lip split. I moved forward. Charlie put an arm out to ward me off.

'Patrick, eh?' he said. 'Well now, laddie. You could just get to be the new *Saint* Patrick. How does that grab you?'

I leaned against his outstretched arm. 'Charlie! For God's sake, man ...'

He didn't mean it, of course. It was all part of the act. But his back-handed swipe caught me off balance, and I went down. I went down hard. My back hit a sharp corner of the safe, and I fell sideways with my knee bent the wrong way. There was nothing phoney about my grunt of pain, and for a few seconds I just lay there gasping. The priest stared at us bug-eyed, his face as white as his collar. Charlie turned back to him and shoved the short barrel of the S&W all the way into his mouth. He gagged, and Charlie smiled.

'Well, what about it?'

'Yes ... no ... I mean, I don't know. There would need to be dispensation ... the

Cardinal . . .'

'F— the Cardinal!' Charlie bunched both lapels of the priest's wet raincoat in one strong hand and yanked the man to his feet. The priest started to tremble violently. His whole body literally shook with terror. His face was slack with fear and wet with perspiration. He was quite incapable of uttering a word. I got to my feet, and this time I wasn't fooling. I jumped between them, slamming the priest back down into the chair. I turned on Charlie.

'All right, that's enough . . .'

Charlie switched the S&W to his left fist, and swung back with his right. His face held something terrible.

'You going to get out of the bloody road, or do I have to knock you out?'

I stood there in the middle, arms outstretched. Just like the man on the wall, and I knew right then how he must have felt. 'Christ, Charlie,' I said, 'you can't . . .'

Charlie let me have it under the heart, and nobody ever hit me any harder. Next thing I knew I was down on my knees with a chest full of fire and my throat filled with bile. As I knelt there, retching, Charlie was back at the priest.

'Now spit it out, you Irish bastard!'

Maybe they don't make martyrs any more. Perhaps people are no longer that stupid. In any event, the priest was not of that number. He told Charlie what he wanted to know, and he told it so fast that Charlie had to make him slow down. By the time I was back on my feet and breathing normally again, Charlie was through with him.

'All right, Farrow. Get him outside and see him on his way. I've got some phoning to do.'

I knew what he meant. Simmonds was big enough to render us normal assistance, but this was different. Authority to cover up on the Jowysz thing would need to come from none less than the Man himself. I knew I would probably be required later to submit to a formal trial, anyway. Right now, though, it wasn't a problem. As Charlie started to dial, I got the priest up out of the chair. Outside, it had stopped raining. At the gate, the priest put his hand on my arm.

'My son...'

'Sorry, chum,' I shook his hand off, 'but I'm not your son, either. Go home. When the police come to ask you about Jowysz, just tell it the way it happened. On you go now.'

I watched him walk away, head bent. The deserted pavement gleamed wetly in the light from the streetlamps. Passing cars were still few and far between. After a little while I went back into the church. Charlie was kneeling by the body. It looked, in the woman's clothing, ugly and grotesque. Charlie was going carefully through seams and pockets. When I came in, he looked up.

116

'Nothing,' he said. 'Not a bloody thing. Clean as a whistle.'

'What now?' I said.

He wiped his hands on the twisted skirt, and stood up. 'We get to hell out of this, before the bobbies arrive. What they don't officially see, they don't officially know. By the time they get around to you . . .'

'Get around to *me*?'

'Yes, you.' Charlie looked at me blandly. 'You *are* the one who let him have it, aren't you?'

I opened my mouth to say something angry, then changed my mind. 'Oh thanks,' I said instead. 'Thank you very bloody much. I hope I can do the same for you some time.'

If he got my meaning, he gave no sign. He nodded, took one last look around the place and headed for the door. 'Come on, then,' he said, 'or they'll be picking you up at the scene of the crime, as they say.'

In the car, he fell silent. Once, when we stopped at a traffic light, I turned my head and caught him looking down at the upturned palms of his hands. I touched his sleeve. 'Charlie . . .' I said.

He did not look at me. 'Shut up,' he said very quietly. 'Just shut up.'

I learned a long time later that Charlie's middle name was Thomas, and that one of his sisters was a nun.

We parked the car not far from the police station, and Charlie got out to use a public telephone. He made an anonymous report about the Jowysz shooting, told the police where to find him, and we got to the station just in time to see a car get on its way. No flashing light or screaming sirens, but enough tyre squeal to make up for both. A C.I.D. sergeant, the one I'd pushed over up on Outlane Moor, let us into our little room and said he would organise a pot of tea. Just, I supposed, to show that he was not holding anything against me. I could have done with something a little more substantial, but I knew without needing to ask that Charlie wouldn't be in the mood for it. He wanted to review our progress.

'If you ask me,' I said, 'I'd say we were back where we started. I'm sorry about Jowysz, Charlie. I *did* try to crease him.'

'Forget it,' Charlie dismissed my apology with an impatient wave of his hand. Then he surprised me by adding something human. 'All things considered, you did pretty well to hit him at all.'

'Yeah,' I said, 'but where did it get us?'

We talked about it. Both of us were sure that Chisholm was the rotten apple. Charlie thought young Sutcliffe had been killed because he knew something, probably without realising it, that would point to Chisholm as the fly in the Fylingdales ointment. Something, perhaps,

118

which would come out under questioning. I said I'd go along with that, but wondered how the killing had been arranged, and by whom. Charlie shook his head.

'Well, we know it wasn't Chisholm, and I don't think somehow it was Jowysz. He was too old, and he didn't have that kind of beef. Sutcliffe was a big strong lad. Whoever pulled him out of his boat and held him down in the water long enough to drown him was no medium-built fifty-year-old. It was probably the driver of the Jowysz car. Question, if they are using the normal three-man-cell system, is whether Chisholm is a part of it. If so, there's only one more we don't know. If not, there's two of the buggers.'

'You don't suppose old man Chisholm's over here, do you?'

'Who? The first of the great defectors? No, I don't think he's here. Else why all that production to get his wife away? Besides there would be too much chance of his being recognised. No. There's another of the sods.'

'Somebody at the Polish Club?'

'I doubt that,' Charlie shook his head. 'I doubt it very much. They'd never put all of their eggs in that or any other kind of basket. You might take a look at the place, though. Find out if Jock *was* there.'

I took a pull at my tea, and stared down into the dark brown dregs. 'I was wondering about it myself. How could old Jock let himself be caught like that? How did Jowysz get him to go up there on the moor in the first place? I'm damned if I can think how ... oh, hell. I don't suppose it matters much, now.'

'That's right. We may never know. So don't let's get carried away on the wrong track. We've got one positive lead.'

'We have?' I said. 'What's that?'

'The old grandma,' said Charlie. He was working on his cuticles with a steel nail file. He looked up. 'Young Chisholm is fond of her. Very fond indeed. Now that he's blown, he'll have to scarper. Oh, he's probably looking forward to joining the proud parents at some idyllic little *dacha* on the Black Sea, but the old lady is no chicken. He knows he'll never see her again.'

'So?' I was ahead of him, really, but he had paused expectantly and I fed him the cue.

'So he might come back to tell her goodbye.'

'You think that's likely? It's a hell of a risk.'

'Yes, I know.' Charlie nodded, and bent over the surplus skin around the edges of his right thumbnail. 'But you've seen him. If he's the sort of cocky little bastard you say he is that kind of gesture would be right in character. Well, wouldn't it?'

'All right then, it's a possibility. So why isn't somebody watching the old lady?'

Charlie finished his surgery on the thumb,

120

and pocketed his nail file. He drained the rest of his tea, and pushed the mug away. 'Somebody is,' he said. 'I just thought the other, the Jowysz thing, was...' He hesitated, searching for the word, and I knew he was thinking about Jock. '... was most urgent. We couldn't be in two places at once, could we?'

'No. Is Simmonds helping, then? He's being damned good to us, isn't he?'

Charlie shrugged. 'He's had his orders. I only hope his boys are as good as he says they are. If we miss Chisholm, or if he doesn't come, we're more or less knackered. Well'—he broke off and looked at his nice fresh manicure—'you'd better get away if you're going to take a look at that club place.'

'What, *now*?'

'Yes, now,' Charlie's bland gaze swung to the clock on the wall above the boarded-up fireplace, and mine followed it. My God, only quarter to ten. I'd been thinking unconsciously that it must be near midnight. I got up and put my coat on. Charlie watched as I broke open the S&W to check that the hammer was resting on an empty chamber, and that the next in line was a full one. He nodded. 'That's the way, and don't hesitate. You might as well be hung for a sheep as for a lamb. Use Bazcyk.'

'Bazcyk?'

'That's right, Bazcyk. How else were you going to get into the joint? Better hurry up,

121

before the old man goes to bed.'

Good old Charlie. Right back in form. My own fault for letting him kid me, even temporarily, that he was human like the rest of us. I went to get the Cortina and drove out to Almondbury. The doctor was still up and about, but he was wearing slippers and an old cardigan and his housekeeper was boiling milk for the Horlicks. I told him what I wanted, spun a load of old cods about why, and asked him what about it. I don't think I fooled him any, but he said O.K. The housekeeper didn't like his going out again, even when I promised to have him back home in not much more than half an hour. But old Bazcyk got into shoes and an overcoat, and we were away.

Some of the lights were on in the church, and there was a police car parked outside. If Bazcyk noticed it, he made no comment. I was just glad there was no ambulance around. That must have been and gone. We passed on by, and I slowed down as we approached the club. There were several cars parked at the kerb, and I swung hard over to stop at a clear space on the other side of the road. I left the doors unlocked.

The club was just a biggish old house with a double front and a door in the middle. Bazcyk knocked, and we were admitted. The little bloke who opened the door clasped the old man to his bosom and greeted him with a staccato splutter of what I supposed was Polish. Bazcyk smiled and introduced me, in English, as a friend of his. We were ushered in. Somewhere upstairs, a piano tinkled, and there were sounds of singing.

The wall between the two big ground-floor rooms on the left side of the house had been knocked down to make one big lounge. Here it was quieter. There was a small bar built against one corner at the rear, and next to it a row of three one-armed bandits. The rest of the room was filled with small tables, and a few neat sofas. The walls were hung with old photographs of groups of men in funny uniforms. There were two chess games going, each with its little knot of critical observers. Most were middle-aged pipe-smokers, and the air in the big room was heavy with tobacco fug. Some of the men looked across as we made our way to the bar, and Bazcyk returned their greetings with smiles and waves. He seemed like a popular old guy. I took the pint he bought for me, and gestured with it at a cluster of framed photographs hanging beside the bar.

'Is Mr. Jowysz on any of these?'

The old man shot me a shrewd look, took a small sip at his whisky, and hoisted his narrow shoulders. 'I don't know, my friend. Let us take a look...'

We moved around, looking at photographs. The doctor paused by some of them to point out his particular cronies and to tell little stories of their deeds and misdeeds. I was conscious, as we moved around the room, of curious stares. We did a complete circuit, studied every face. That of Jowysz was not among them. Old Bazcyk was mildly surprised.

'That's strange. Most of the older members were in one or another of these units. I wonder . . .'

'Oh, it doesn't matter.' I shrugged it off. 'It's just that a photograph might have helped us in our enquiries. He's still missing, you know.'

'Wait a minute'—we were sitting now at a table to the right of the door—'if it's a likeness you want, I think I can help you. Jowysz was with me in our chess team when we won the Northern Clubs trophy. Yes, I'm sure he was. We had a photograph taken, and I think I've still got mine at home. Would you like to borrow it?'

I said I would, and he promised to look it out when I took him back to Almondbury. I finished my beer, and insisted on paying for the next one myself. The old man didn't want another drink, so I took my pint pot back to the bar and hoped the steward would not make a fuss about taking cash from a non-member. He didn't, and I had time as he was drawing the ale to take another look at the place. Both chess games seemed now to be moving to a climax, and most of the men left in the lounge were pressed around the tables. What noise there was

124

came from the two who were playing the slot machines. They were feeding coins into the things as though this was the very last day that money was ever going to be any good. They were of the younger set and their comments, often ribald, came out explosively in an odd-sounding mixture of guttural Polish and homely old Yorkshire. I paid for my pint, took a little sup to obviate spillage, and moved back to our table. I'd just got seated when the priest came in.

He was with a husky young bloke in a zippered jerkin and corduroy slacks. They seemed to be deep in talk and, at first, he did not see me. They made their way between the tables to the bar, and the young bloke bought the priest a Scotch. It looked like a large one. Then he moved over to talk with the two who were playing the bandits, and the priest turned his back on the bar to look around the room. That's when he saw me. He turned round quickly, and watched me in the bottle-fronted mirror at the back of the bar. I drank up my beer and touched the old doctor on the arm. I thought it best to get him out of there.

'All right, Dr. Bazcyk, I'd better get you back home. That housekeeper of yours will be after my blood.'

The old man smiled, and rose. In the hall I helped him with his overcoat. When the little chap on the door opened up for us, we were hit in the face by a spatter of rain. The weather was back to normal. The road was busy now with the turn-out of pubs and movies traffic, and we had to wait a while before we could cross the road. The car was still there. It had to be. There was a big fat policeman standing guard on it. I had forgotten to leave the side-lights on.

'This your car, sir?'

I got out my wallet and let him sneak a glimpse at the etching. He stroked the side of his nose. We both knew that he was supposed to nick me regardless. He hesitated, then reached for his notebook. Across the road people were coming out of the club and running through the rain for their cars. I got the old man into the Cortina and turned to the bobby.

'Look,' I said. 'You know Inspector Simmonds?' He nodded. 'Yes, mate,' I went on, 'and so do I. So don't make me have to tell him that your bloody stupidity ballsed up the job I'm on. All right?'

He stepped back at that, and started to let me off with a warning about not forgetting in future to observe the regulations. Before he'd half done, I was away. The doctor did not speak on the way back to his home. He seemed thoughtful. I hoped he was as clean as Charlie and I had him pegged for. I got out at the house and went with him up to the front door. He rang the bell and we waited, huddled into the porch to avoid the driving rain. Soon, the porch light snapped on, and the old lady asked us querulously from behind the fast closed door who it was at this time of night. Bazcyk told her, and she opened up with a great rattle of bolts and chains. I stood in the hall whilst the doctor went to fetch the photograph he'd promised, and the old dear glowered disapprovingly as the water ran off my raincoat and on to her nice clean carpet. Old Bazcyk was back in surprisingly short time with a postcard-size print of the chess team. Of the six, only he really looked the part. Which, I suppose, must go to show something or other but I don't know quite what. I put the photo into my inside pocket, declined his offer of a drink, and bid them good night. The housekeeper closed the door on me with what I thought was unnecessary force.

I walked back down the short dark drive, taking care not to brush against the rain-laden rhododendrons. This time I'd left the sidelights on. Somebody big was leaning with his back against the door on the driver's side. There was not enough light from the street-lamps for me clearly to see his face, but he looked definitely familiar.

'You one of the fellers what was down at the church tonight?'

I spun round a fraction too late. The one behind me let go with something hard, and I did not get my arm up quick enough. He caught me high on the shoulder, near the neck, and I staggered across the drive away from him. A third one was closing in from the other side, but he was a slow mover. I swung my right arm round like a flail, and got him full in the face with the edge of my hand. The one they'd been hardening for me at the house up in Scotland. I thought I felt some teeth go, and he fell back against the gatepost with a muffled yell of pain. The first one launched himself up off the car and came at me fast with what looked like an axe-handle.

If number two had not been quite so eager to get once more into the act, it might have been all over there and then. But he followed up with a rush, and his mate with the axe-handle was forced to dodge around looking for room to get one in. I took a fist or something on the side of the head, and my ear sang like a siren. I kicked out sideways and caught a shin. Then the axe-handle fell, and the fireworks exploded. I reeled back against the rhododendrons, clutching wildly at the wet branches in an effort to stay upright. The axe-handle man closed in again, and started to chop about viciously in the half-dark. If they survived, Bazcyk's bushes would need no pruning for years. I ducked away from under and swung savagely for his guts. I wasn't worrying about any beltline and he fell back, when I landed a hard one, with a gasp of agony.

But the others had rallied now and were crowding me hard. We thrashed around in the shrubbery, cursing and swinging. They pushed me backwards through the soaking bushes, and I felt my shoulder blades up against some kind of fence. It sagged perilously as one of them slammed me back against it with a fist to the cheek-bone, and I dropped to my knees in the churned wet soil as another of them split my skull with his little plaything. Then two of them held me while the other one, him whose teeth would never be the same again, vented his spite. I saw his knee coming up and threw my leg across, but he hurt me bad all the same. He closed in, spitting a shower of blood and oaths out of his broken mouth, and started slugging. Every one felt like he was using a sledge-hammer. Once, his fist hit the butt of the S&W, and that one hurt him as much as it hurt me. But it didn't stop him, and pretty soon I started not to care about what they were doing to me. I was going under.

Suddenly, there was a lot more light all over the place, and I heard someone yelling. They let go of me, and I fell down flat with my face in the wet earth. I was dimly aware that they were running away, and tried to push myself up to my knees. Someone bent over me, and I covered my head with my arm. But the hand was a gentle one.

'Elsie! Elsie! Telephone for the police—quickly!'

It was Bazcyk. He helped me up, and I shook my ringing head. My face felt very wet, and it was too warm to be just rain. Some of whatever it was spattered off on the doctor's white shirt, and then I *knew* it wasn't just rain. I clutched at his arm.

'No! No police. Tell her to stop. I don't want the police. Just help me ... just help...'

The two old people helped me inside, and if the housekeeper thought I'd made a mess on her carpet the first time, God knows what she felt then. Bazcyk struggled me on to the couch in his surgery, and got down quickly to a survey of the damage. He loosed a splutter of Polish. The housekeeper hovered at his back, wringing her hands and clucking like an old hen. He silenced her sternly, and set her to fetching swabs and stitching gear and basins of hot water. He worked over me with speed and skill, shaking his head and tut-tutting softly all the while.

'My God, man. What have they done to you? Who were they? Do you know them? Good heavens ... look at that—they could have killed you! Why should they do this terrible thing? How did they know you were here?'

He swabbed and cleaned and probed and stitched and his busy little needle hurt like hell. He put three stitches into the gash over my cheek-bone, just under the eye, and every one hurt worse than the blow which caused it. Then he shaved off what seemed like half of my hair, and started on my skull. Not quite so bad as he'd thought, he said. Only four sutures needed to close it up nicely. He wanted to go on then with a search for bruised or broken ribs, but I'd started to feel almost human again and said thank you, but no. I was all right in that area. It was a lie, but I got up off the couch under my own steam and managed, by a great effort of will, to make the room stop spinning. When I'd got it—the room—to slow right down, I asked Bazcyk please to give me my jacket and raincoat.

When he had gone to get them, I remembered the S&W. I took it out of my waistband and put it into my trousers pocket. Too late, of course. He must have seen it. But if he had, and if he missed it as he helped me on with my coats, he made no sign. In the hall he held out his hand. As I shook it, he smiled sadly.

'There are those,' he said, nodding, 'who imagine foolishly that our struggles ended in 1945. I wish you to know that I am not one of them. Take care, young man. You may not always be quite so lucky...'

I opened my mouth to ask him what made him so sure that I was one of the goodies, then closed it again. What the hell. I thanked him as best I knew how for his enormous help and he let me persuade him, although of course he knew a damn' sight better, that I was fit to take the Cortina. I eased myself into the driving seat, rested my reeling head for a few seconds against the rim of the steering wheel, then switched on the ignition. I was one big throbbing pain. If the car had been wired for effect, and I'd been blown to kingdom come, the blast would have brought nothing but sweet relief. As it was, I was fated to survive. I got to a phone box. I seemed to be spending the best part of my life, when I wasn't being beaten up, getting to a phone box. Charlie, thank God, was still at the police station.

'Farrow? Where the hell have you been?'

I closed my eyes and counted, quite slowly, to ten. Then, taking care not to get excited, I told him. If he had interrupted, or made just one of his bloody remarks, I'd have blown my aching top. But he didn't. Not Charlie. He just listened without comment until I was all through.

'Are you sure it was the youths from the club?'

'Yes,' I said tiredly, 'I told you. I'm positive.'

'You mean they beat you up simply and solely on account of the priest thing?'

'Yes,' I said. 'On account of the priest thing. But it's all right, Charlie. Be my guest.'

There was a short silence while he gave it thought. Then he said he supposed I had better call it a day. He suggested a warm bath to ease the bruising, and so to bed. I thanked him. I thanked him very kindly.

WEDNESDAY

Charlie was right about the bath. I woke up next morning feeling a lot better than I had any right to feel. My face and head were very sore, and I was going to have to wear sunglasses for a week or so, but apart from that I felt great. Then I tried to get out of bed.

It took me rather longer than usual, and I decided somewhere along the way that my regular daily dozen could go by the board today. I shaved gingerly, eased into my clothes, and totted up the damage. I looked as though I'd gone fifteen rounds with Henry Cooper, with all my clothes on in a muddy field. I did what I could for the suit, ate a fair old breakfast to make up for the supper I hadn't had last night, and went out to meet Charlie. He was waiting for me in the Cortina, and looked like he'd been there for hours. As I climbed in beside him, he glanced pointedly at his watch. I just ignored the gesture. It must have been all of eleven minutes past eight.

'Yes ...' he was looking at my face, 'they really worked you over, didn't they? You'd better get yourself a pair of dark glasses.'

'Funny you should say that,' I said. 'Do you think it's a fair case for expenses?'

He hesitated, the humourless bastard, then nodded.

'Yes, all right then,' he agreed. 'But there's no need . . .'

'I know,' I interrupted. 'I know. There's no need to go mad. I'll try to remember, Charlie. Honest I will. Now, what's new?'

'Yes, well, Eldon's disappeared. That's what's new.'

'Eldon? Christ, don't tell me he's in this too! What happened?'

'Landlady says he got a telephone call late last night from his girl friend Linda Butterworth. About eleven o'clock. She—the landlady—is quite sure it really was the girl friend as she—the girl friend—has telephoned often. Eldon had gone to bed. Landlady got him up. Eldon very agitated, told landlady that his grandmother had been knocked down in the street by a motor car, and seriously injured. He dressed at once, said he was not sure how long he'd be gone, and took off in his car.'

'The call was a phoney?'

'Right, so far as the accident part is concerned. Old Mrs Peacock—that's Eldon's granny—was fit as a fiddle at seven ack emma this very morning. Never been knocked down in her life.'

'And Eldon?'

'Disappeared. The old thin-air trick. Last person to see him was the landlady. He left Whitby around twenty past eleven, headed for his grandma's place in Oldham. You know the route. Somewhere along it, something happened to him. Unless, of course, he never intended going to Oldham anyway.'

'If that's so, why all the performance with the girl friend? Why not just up and away?'

'Good question,' said Charlie. 'Except that we're not sure yet it *was* the girl friend.'

'Well,' I said, 'there's only one way to find out.'

'Right again.' Charlie nodded. He patted me on the knee, and I thought for a moment he was actually going to smile. 'But try not to be too long about it, Farrow. I've got a funny feeling in my water that things are starting to hot up. How long will it take you to get over there?'

'You mean how long will it take just to get there? Or how long will it take to get there, find the girl, talk to her, maybe see the granny...'

'All right, all right. How long's it going to take you?'

'I'd say about dinner time.'

'Dinner-time!'

'You wouldn't want me to fill you with false hopes.'

I calculated that this, if Charlie was running true to form, would be the point at which he'd

135

abdicate. I'd got the message, he'd made his point, and all the rest from here on in was superfluous chat. Sure enough, he flung his door open and got out of the car. As I was sliding painfully into the driver's seat, he stuck his head in at the window.

'Oh, and Farrow'—he said—'can't you do anything about that suit? I think we might run to a clothes brush . . .'

'Bollocks,' I said. But I don't think he heard me. He had turned quickly on his heel and was away.

I stopped at a garage in town to fill up the Cortina, taking care to get a receipt for the £1.66 I had spent on the Section's behalf. The pump attendant asked me if I wanted stamps *as well*, and I let him intimidate me into making him a present of them. There was a brave sun as I ran over the top, and Outlane Moor looked harmless and peaceful. I thought, as I passed the deserted lane end, of old Jock. I wondered if he had any family, and about the funeral. These thoughts depressed me and I forced myself to stop, because it was against all the rules. Then I told myself to hell with the rules, because not to have done would have made me just like Charlie. Which set me thinking in turn about Charlie, and I knew deep down in my guts that he was the one who had it right.

It was a little early for the heavy stuff, and the narrow road across the moors was fairly clear. I made the run to Oldham in just under the half-hour. Then as I dropped on to the long steep hill running down into town, I realised I did not have the girl's address. I'd just have to get it from the granny. *Maude Peacock, née Edwards, born Royton, Lancs., 1900.* Address—Christ! I didn't have the old lady's address, either. What a way to run a railroad. Sod it, I'd have to phone Charlie. He was going to love that. No, wait ... Charlie had told me the girl's name. Butterworth. Linda Butterworth. And I seemed to remember thinking for some reason that she was on the phone at home. Worth a try, anyway.

That knock on the head last night must have scrambled my brains. I tried several Butterworth, L. numbers before it tumbled to me that the phone was probably listed under her father's name. God, there were dozens of them. I left the phone booth and found a tobacconist-cum-everything, bought an ounce of Escudo and a cheap pair of sunglasses, and got the bloke to give me change in tanners for the fifty-pence piece. When I finally struck lucky, I had just two left. But it wasn't just the money. I'd wasted nearly half an hour.

'Mrs. Butterworth? Can I speak to your Linda, please?' Then, just to make sure, 'It's about Stanley—Stanley Eldon...'

'Oh, yes! How's Mrs. Peacock—his grandma—have you heard? Is Stanley all right?

We thought he might have come home to see our Linda this morning before she went off to school . . .'

'Off to school?'

'Yes, they don't break up for the holidays till next week, you know.'

I got it out of her that Linda was a teacher at Marlborough Street Infants' School. She had left home early that morning in order to call at the Peacock house, expecting to see Stanley there. Wasn't it awful about old Mrs. Peacock . . .

I said it was, thanked her, and rang off. My chum in the tobacconist's shop didn't know off-hand where Marlborough Street was, but he had a street map in the stock and he looked it up for me. Just my luck, it was way over on the Manchester side. I drove down to the bottom of the hill, turned right at the Co-op, and made my tortuous way up through the town. Marlborough Street Infants' was one of those tall, old, grim and grimy stone-built schools best described by Charles Dickens. Curiously, the kids seemed to mind it not at all. Great wild bunches of them fought and screamed and tore around the pitted playground like bats out of hell. As I drew up by the green-painted iron railings surrounding the place, a bell clanged. I watched the kids form up, pushing and jostling, into three long straggling lines. The ranks converged at the great arched doorway and were drawn, like some great writhing snake, into its maw. When all but the last few snivelling stragglers were safely inside I felt it secure to get out of the car.

The young woman who asked me in the carbolic-smelling corridor what it was I wanted looked barely old enough to have graduated from the place, let alone teach in it. When I asked for Miss Butterworth she wrinkled her pert nose and scratched behind her ear. It turned out that her friend Miss Butterworth, who taught 2b, would be busy with her first class and did not have a free period until after playtime. I told her it was very important that I see her friend, and solicited any suggestion. She said she would ask the Head if it was all right for her to swap her own free period, which was now, and would I like to wait in the common room. I told her that, if it was all right, I'd rather see Miss Butterworth outside. She said O.K. then, make it in the playground.

Linda Butterworth was a very nice girl, but not of the brightest echelons. If Eldon or someone else did not marry her she would be teaching in the Infants' department all of her life. But having regard to what she had going for her, such a fate was unlikely. She was tall for a girl, had a lovely heart-shaped face, and was bountifully endowed in all the right places. Her large blue eyes were thickly fringed with her very own lashes, and her fair hair shone with good health. I wondered what the Head thought about the length, or lack of it, of her skirt. She looked worried.

'Did you want to see me?'

'Miss Butterworth? Yes. I'm James Clark'—I held out my hand—'a colleague of Stanley's. How d'you do.'

'A colleague? What's happened to him? Is he all right?'

'Well, yes, we think so,' I said soothingly. 'But someone seems to be playing some kind of silly joke on him . . .'

'Silly!' She was angry now, and that was better. 'I'd say it was more than silly. It was absolutely stupid!'

'I know. You're quite right. And we're trying to get to the bottom of it. Tell me—what happened last night?'

She was just getting ready for bed when the phone rang. Her father answered it, and shouted upstairs that it was someone for her. She came down in her dressing gown, thinking it must be Stanley phoning to apologise for the row they'd had when he was over at the weekend. But it wasn't Stanley, it was someone she didn't know. A man. He said he was a neighbour of Mrs. Peacock's, and was phoning to tell her that the old lady had been knocked down in Oldham after coming out of the pictures . . .

'Didn't you think it strange at all that the
140

neighbour should get in touch with you? Why couldn't he ring Stanley direct?'

'Well, no ... I mean, I don't know. No, not really. Old Mrs. Peacock loved to talk, you know. The neighbours knew everything about Stanley, including all about me. Then, I mean, there's nobody else, is there? Stanley's all she's got left now, what with the rest of them being in America. And it's easier to phone a local number. It's a lot cheaper, too,' she added sagely.

'Yes, I suppose you're right,' I said. 'Tell me, though—did this chap actually *ask* you to telephone Stanley, or was that your own idea?'

'Do you know, I couldn't really say, now that you ask. But it's the sort of thing you'd do anyway, isn't it? I mean, naturally ... oh, if ever I get my hands on whoever it was, I'll ... I'll ...'

'Yes, I know how you feel, Miss Butterworth. But tell me something else, when did you find out that the old lady was all right?'

'This morning, of course.' She put up a slim hand to sweep the hair from her eyes, and the pale blue jumper tightened across her firm young breasts. Then, catching my eye, she blushed hotly and folded her arms across them. 'I left the house a bit earlier than usual so that I could look in at Mrs. Peacock's on my way down to school—to find out how she was. I figured that Stan would be there, you see. If he

141

wasn't at the hospital, that is. But there was old Mrs. Peacock herself, large as life, and right as rain! You could have knocked me down with a feather!'

I turned my head after getting into the car, and caught her staring after me. She'd already been worried. Now she looked puzzled, too. It might have been the dark glasses, and the parts they were not quite big enough to hide. I was willing to bet she could hardly wait to get home and tell her folks about it. I had left her abruptly just as she was getting around to asking where Stanley was now. As I let out the clutch, I saw in the mirror that she was running across the playground to catch me at the corner. Instead of going back the way I had come, I carried straight on and went all around the district to get back on to the main road. Not that it mattered, but I hoped she did not realise I'd done it just to avoid her.

My head ached, my face was sore, and my body felt as though I'd just gone the distance with Cassius Clay. I tooled the Cortina down through the town centre, straight out on to the Huddersfield Road, and turned off at the Co-op to take the Ripponden Road. Anybody who follows the signposts to get from Oldham to Huddersfield, please take note. Apart from all the other advantages, there is a little café up there in Denshaw which makes a cup of coffee very well worth stopping for. The home-made

142

jam pastry is pretty good too. I had one of each and then, because I had saved time by not bothering to go and see the grandmother, I had the same again.

Climbing out of Denshaw, I came up against a convoy of heavies. Seven or eight of them, spread well out and labouring up the twisting gradient in low gear. Nothing for it, on that road, but to get in the queue and try to think pleasant thoughts on the long slow way to the top. Once past the summit, there are one or two fairly long straight stretches where, luck and oncoming traffic permitting, it is possible to leap-frog and get away. I dropped into second, closed all the windows against the vile exhaust fumes from the tanker in front, and settled back to think about Eldon.

It looked on the face of it as though the others had got him. But why, what would be the point? Chisholm was blown now—why burden themselves with Eldon? Assuming, of course, that they hadn't just killed him. But why kill him—unless he was in some way mixed up with them. A definite possibility, in spite of Charlie's not much liking the idea. These and other thoughts chased themselves around the various aches nagging at my poor sore head, and I realised suddenly that we were over the top and cruising across the first of the flats along the moorland ridge. I gunned the motor and passed the tanker and the brick lorry in front of him in one long hop. Then there was a stream of stuff coming the other way, and I had to wait. I was just about to pass the last of the convoy on my side when it forked off left to take the road for Elland. It was a relief to see some open road in front of the bonnet, and I put my foot down.

It happened when I was doing over eighty on that last long straight coming up to Nont Sarah's. I heard a shattering crash, and the windscreen turned instantly into an opaque mass of tiny cracks. The sudden terrific shock made me screw up my eyes, and I felt rather than heard the frantic scrabbling of my nearside tyres as the spinning wheels tore at the loose gravel at the edge of the road. I resisted the screaming impulse to wrench the wheel hard over, then the training started to pay off. I held straight and braked hard. Almost before the drums had stopped screeching, I had jerked on the handbrake, slapped the gear lever into neutral, and hurled myself across the car to snatch at the opposite door handle. As I got it open, the second shot hit. The bullet smashed another hole in the spider-webbed windscreen and passed over my shoulder to smack into the seat squab. I threw myself clear of the car and rolled head-first into the wide ditch flanking the road. When I came up, with the S&W in my fist, I had the car between me and whoever it was.

The Cortina's nearside wheels were off the edge of the paved road and both were within inches of dropping into the ditch. The ditch was about three feet deep, and I was kneeling in as many inches of water which lay in the bottom of it. My head and shoulders were covered by the front wheel. I eased forward until I could see past it. The road beyond was empty all the way up to Nont Sarah's, at least three hundred yards away. Opposite the old stone pub, on the other side of the road, was a row of derelict cottages. Nothing more than a tumble of ancient stones. Just the far side of these, several little-used lanes led at fairly close intervals off the main road right and left. Those on the left ran down to Elland, those on the right into Golcar and Milnsbridge. I could see no movement; nothing. Then a car came up over the top from Huddersfield, passed Nont Sarah's, and headed out towards me doing about sixty. A Vauxhall. He slowed down only slightly as he passed the Cortina, and I saw a woman in the passenger seat stare curiously out of the side window. The Vauxhall did not stop. Nor did the Hillman which followed soon afterwards, or the Bedford van after that. Your Englishman's capacity for minding his own damn business. I watched and waited and nothing happened. No more shots, no more nothing. Then a car passed going in the Huddersfield direction. Still nothing.

When I heard the approaching rumble of the last of the heavies I had passed back there along the top, I climbed carefully up out of the ditch and crouched behind the wide-open nearside door. The lorry driver slowed right down to take an inquisitive shufty as he swerved to pass, and I scrambled in. I slapped into second gear, let go the handbrake, and shot forward right up tight into his back end. I was holding the wheel in my left hand and battering away at the windscreen with the butt of the Smith & Wesson. I managed to smash out most of the cracked and useless glass long before we reached the derelict cottages, and by that time was ready for anything. I held the Cortina's bonnet right in under the lorry's tail until I knew we must be within spitting distance of the cottages, then dropped back just enough to let me swing out fast.

If there had been anything coming up smartly the other way it would have been that's all for now. As it was, the driver of the Austin 1100 saw me in time to jump on his brakes, and I caught a glimpse of his outraged face as I threw the Ford across the road in front of him and into the littered yard of the ruined houses. I heard him screech to a stop, and that was good. Whoever I was after couldn't kill everybody, and wouldn't even want to try. I drove the Cortina lurching and bumping across the yard and catapulted out of it and into cover. As I crouched beside the corner of the old buildings with the S&W in my fist, I heard the Austin driver yell. When I turned my head, I saw that the lorry had turned into the forecourt at Nont Sarah's, and that the driver was climbing down out of the cab. Then another car stopped. The famous English reserve had finally broken down. It looked like we were going to have a regular party. As the first one came towards me, I slipped the gun into the side pocket of my jacket and stood up.

'Here! What the bloody hell's goin' on, like?'

He was red in the face. By the look of the broken veins decorating the façade of his marvellous nose, he was probably always red in the face. But he was mad, all right. He flung an arm out to point back at his Austin.

'That's a bloody new motor, tha knows. None o' yer bloody firm's cars, neither. Cost me bloody nearly a thousand quid, that did! I've never seen nowt like it—bloody nearly smashed the bugger to smithereens! What's t'bloody game, like?'

'It's a'reyt for thee,' I said. 'But what's tha think about this lot?'

I gestured at my wet and filthy suit, and at the Cortina's shattered windscreen. He viewed the damage, and calmed down a bit. We were joined by the lorry driver and the man from the second car, and I told the story I had decided on, making up the detail as I went along.

'Bloody kids,' I said. 'Kids or bloody maniacs. I saw them just before it happened. I must've been doing eighty. Windscreen blew up. Air rifle, I reckon. Murderous little bastards! I could easy have been killed!'

It was obvious that none of them knew anything about the range and power of air rifles, though the lorry driver did look vaguely sceptical and said he wondered if it could have been a stone off the road. But the Austin driver, forgetting his own grievance in favour of the much bigger one that was mine, was indignantly sure I was right. They helped me search all three of the roof-and-window-less ruins, then advised me in concert to tell the police. I said I would, and eventually they drove away. I pretended to be picking the last shards of glass out of the windscreen. When they had gone I went back into the ruins, knelt by the empty window-frame on the end gable, and picked up the two empty .22 calibre shell cases I'd previously kicked under a pile of old laths.

I drove the Cortina down into town and left it at the Ford main dealers for repair. They said they would whip a new windscreen in by tomorrow, or Friday morning at latest, and I told them that was fine. I got a few funny looks both there and at the multiple tailor's, but they both accepted my accident story because why the hell should they not. The tailor rigged me out in a suit which fitted slightly better, if anything, than the one I had ruined. The shop sold shirts, but not socks and underwear. I told them to put suit and shirt into a carton, and I'd take them with me. I paid with my credit card, and went out in search of the rest of my wardrobe. I bought shoes, and all. Charlie *would* be pleased.

I then went straight back to the hotel, had a bath, and changed into my brand-new outfit. As I walked down into the lobby to phone Charlie at the police station number, the clock was striking twelve and they were just opening the cocktail bar. So I had a Canadian Club before I phoned because that, just then, was exactly how I felt. Charlie wasn't at the station, but had left a message that I was to leave any number from which I called and he'd ring back. In no ways daunted, I returned to the bar and had another rye. I was just contemplating the wisdom or otherwise of further indulgence when the porter came to ask if I was Mr. Farrow. I told him I was, and he said there was a telephone call for me.

Charlie did his famous listening act, and said at the end of it that we had better meet up somewhere out of town. I suggested the Three Nuns. He said all right, but that he'd got something to do and would join me there as soon as he could. I walked to the taxi rank in Northumberland Street, took the last cab in line, and got him to drive me out to the Brighouse roundabout. I walked the distance from there to the pub, all three hundred yards of it, because it was a nice day and I needed the exercise. The lass behind the bar in the saloon was pretty mature, but none the worse for that. She told me her name was Sadie, and I bought her a gin and tonic. She served my Canadian Club in a nice glass, with plenty of ice. The stitches in my face were giving me hell.

Charlie walked in just as I was returning from a visit to the Gents'. He looked me over, including the shoes and I knew exactly what he was thinking. But all he said was:

'You're stinking, Farrow. There's liquor on your breath.'

'Not so much as there would have been if it had taken you a little longer to get here. Anyway, what about it? You going to give me the sack?'

He sighed, and I was almost sorry I'd said it. He leaned forward, elbows on the table. The fascinated Sadie brought my drink across, and asked if she could get something for my friend. Charlie opened his mouth, and I told her to get him a bitter lemon. We waited until she had served him and was back out of earshot behind the bar. Charlie watched me watch her undulating rump. I slipped my sunglasses off and shot him an exaggerated wink.

'Beautiful hip movement there, Charlie.

Beautiful.'

He blinked slowly and took a pull at his bitter lemon.

'Keep your mind on the bloody job, Farrow. What about this Butterworth girl?'

'Nice,' I said, 'very nice. But I think I'd rather have old Sadie here. More my type, you know?'

He flushed, and I decided then that I had gone far enough. 'Yes, well, I'm sure the Butterworth kid's all right. Somebody just used her rather cleverly to get Eldon away from Whitby and out over here. I'd say it was someone who knew her.'

I told him all about my talk with the girl, and went on to detail the events which had followed. He asked a lot of questions, including the one I was hoping he wouldn't.

'What about the old lady, Eldon's grandma?'

'I didn't get to see her.'

'You *what?*'

'Look, Charlie,' I said. 'What would have been the point of wasting time with the old girl? She's just like the Butterworth kid, for God's sake. She knows sod all. I just thought I'd be better employed getting back where the action is.'

'You did that, all right. And they damn nearly put you right out of it. To get one or both of us up on to that road must have been the object of the whole Eldon exercise.' He made rings on the table with the bottom of the glass. 'Why, though? Why would they go to that kind of trouble?'

'To throw us off,' I said. 'Or to stall us, one of the two. A diversion, maybe. Something to keep us busy.'

'You could be right. Either way we'll have to get rid of the Cortina. They're obviously on to it, or they couldn't have picked you off up there on the moor. It was a .22 you say?'

I took the two little cartridge cases out of my pocket and put them into his hand. He looked at them, then at me.

'Not even magnum.'

'Christ!' I said, 'what do you want—blood? They didn't need to be magnum. He probably thought that all he had to do was hit the windscreen. That's a narrow road, Charlie, and it carries a lot of heavy stuff. I was just lucky there was nothing big anywhere near at the time. He damn nearly put me into the ditch as it was. ...' I stood up annoyed because I'd let him rattle me, and went across to the bar to get myself another drink. He eyed my glass when I came back, and nodded.

'Go easy on that stuff. You've got work to do.'

'What about yourself,' I said sarcastically. 'You had a busy morning, too?'

'So-so,' he said calmly. 'Little Christine Palmer, age seven. Found this morning in the upstairs room of a derelict building in Brighouse. She'd been assaulted.'

'What's that got to do with us?'

'Nothing, except that Simmonds has had to put every available man on the job. We're left with only one, and even he will be taken from us before the day's over. In the meantime he's watching Granny Chisholm.'

'Any movement there?'

'No,' he shook his head. 'But she's not on the phone, and she's had no mail. She's talked to nobody except the neighbours and one or two local shopkeepers.' He looked at his watch. 'You'd better get us something to eat. I want you to take over just before two o'clock, and it's a quarter past one now.'

I got Sadie to organise two rounds of beef and two rounds of cheese and tomato, and went to the Gents' so that Charlie would have to pay for them. I stood in front of the mirror in the little washroom and took off the dark glasses. My face around the eyes looked just like an empty sky at night, all greens and yellows and shading in parts to a dull dark blue. The left cheek, under the cut, was puffed and tender. I felt old and sad and very definitely in the wrong business. When I got back, Charlie was halfway through the sandwiches, and Sadie told me that would be ten-and-sixpence, please. Nine shillings for the sandwiches and one-and-six for another bitter lemon. I gave her a fifty-pence bit, added a tenpenny piece, and told her to keep the change. She said thank you very much and did I want another drink myself. I said bless you no, I was driving. Charlie looked up from his attack on the cheese and tomato, and grunted.

'Better get on with it,' he said. 'Two o'clock at the Majestic cinema. It's Bingo day.'

'Yes, Charlie.' The beef was very good, except that it hurt me to chew. 'I understand perfectly. Bingo day.'

'That's right, Bingo day. Granny Chisholm never misses. Hail, rain, or shine, as they say. So get in early, and pick her up from there. I'll see that you're taken off before eight, even if I have to relieve you myself.'

'Thanks, Charlie,' I said, 'but I wouldn't want you to put yourself out.'

'Not at all.' He finished his share of the sandwiches and shook out a big white handkerchief to work on his hands and face. Then he took out another one and, presumably to give me time to finish my share, polished up his glasses. He got to his feet while I was still trying to swallow my last mouthful. 'You ready?'

He'd got the Rover back, God knows how, and we were into town before I'd forced up the first belch. He let me off in a side street near the cinema and, as I turned to walk away, stuck his head out of the window.

'Oh, and Farrow ...' I stopped and looked back at him. 'If he does show, try not to kill him, eh?' He must have been in gear with his foot on the clutch because he was gone before I could think of something bitter enough to say.

The Huddersfield Majestic had seen better days. They have all seen better days. This one had given up even trying. The carpets were scuffed and torn, and the whole place was permeated with that curious catty smell peculiar to large public places which are never properly cleaned or aired. I paid my ten new pence club-joining fee, another fivepence to enter, and walked down the short dark passage into the auditorium.

The entrances to the balcony were cordoned off. There was no one around, so I stepped over the frayed loop of rope and climbed the stairs two at a time. I had the dress circle all to myself, and chose a seat in the middle of the front row. It had been slashed and repaired, and slashed again. Thinking of my nice new suit I did a quick check for chewing gum. The expense account had taken just about as much punishment as it would stand. I filled a pipe, then changed my mind about lighting it and perhaps drawing attention. Downstairs, it was all starting to happen. The caller was on stage with his several stewards, and they were setting up the props. The first dozen rows of seats were filling up rapidly. Most of the players were

155

women, with here and there the odd man. Courtesy, no doubt, of the National Assistance.

I did not recognise old Mrs. Chisholm at first sight, because I saw her from above and behind and she was wearing a coloured headscarf. Then I saw her in profile as she turned into the third row from the front. There were several empty seats on the row, and she chose one beside a dark stocky man wearing an old flat cap and a muffler. She settled herself down, put on her spectacles and arranged her Bingo cards in proper order. The woman on her right said something to her, and they began a conversation.

Then the caller tapped his microphone and blew into the thing to test it for sound. He switched on his random selector contrivance, and the little numbered balls began to jump around on the air jets inside their perspex container. He checked that his stewards were at their positions in front and to the sides of the stage, announced that the first game would be a full house, and called peremptorily for eyes down. There was a sudden hush. Pencils were poised, and several hundred breaths were bated. And the first number was—wait for it—six and nine—sixty-nine . . .

I sat through two full houses, three games of one line each, and then what they called the snowball. The entertainment progressed in fits of absolute silence, whilst the calling was on, alternating with bursts of uproarious din which broke out as soon as someone called house. The stewards' hoarse shouts of 'Correct ... correct ... correct ...' as they checked off the winning tickets could hardly be heard. The players showed each other their tickets, checked that they had not missed a number, discussed the honesty or otherwise of the officials, and generally made one hell of a racket. After the checking, lucky winners were paid off, eyes down was called, and the noise stopped as though turned off by a tap.

Nobody won the snowball—a sort of continuing competition in which the cash prizes, if not won, are carried forward to swell next week's total. And after the great collective sigh of disappointment, the caller announced an interval. Following all that strain on the emotions, the players needed refreshment. Plump girls paraded the aisles with trays of ices and soft drinks. They even had tea and coffee in plastic containers, and right then I wouldn't have minded a cup. The din was worse than ever. The man on Mrs. Chisholm's left got up, and she put a hand on his arm. He bent his head, presumably to hear what she was saying, then edged his way to the end of the row. I assumed that she was asking him to get her something from one of the salesgirls.

I assumed wrong. He walked past the queue lined up in front of the nearest girl, and made for the double doors to the left of the stage. An illuminated sign above it said GENTS. It also said EXIT. I must admit that I thought even then he was just going about his natural occasions. But he paused with one hand pushing the door, turning half round, and waved. The old lady waved back.

I jumped up and threw a leg over the balcony rail, decided the drop was too much, and turned to run along the front of the seats. I took the stairs in great stumbling bounds, leaped over the rope at the bottom, and tore down the aisle, scattering headscarved women right and left. I battered through the door marked EXIT, slammed into and just as quickly out of the deserted GENTS, and raced down the empty concrete passageway leading to the rear exit and car park. The door at the end of the passage was ajar, and I could see daylight.

I realised afterwards that he must have heard me pounding down that passage after him. I ran straight into it. I had one brief glimpse of the cinema car park, used in the daytime by local trades and business men and so pretty near filled with cars and vans. Then the world exploded in a blaze of stars, and I was engulfed in that one agonised instant of blinding nausea which follows a violent blow on the skull. I do not even remember falling down. How he got my fourteen stone over the tailgate of the covered Bedford truck, God only knows.

Perhaps they were both there. We never found out.

I surfaced slowly, in a muddy sea of pain, unaware, at first, of who or what or where I was. My instinctive reaction was to struggle against a return to consciousness. I wanted to sink back into blank, unfeeling limbo. I had a headache so excruciating it made me feel horribly sick. I opened my eyes, and that was the last straw. Partly digested food rose hot and sour in my throat, and I was wrenched into wakefulness by sudden dizzy panic. My mouth appeared to be sealed up tight, and the rising bile surged like a gusher of warm acid into my sinuses. Seeking an outlet, it flooded the nasal passages and ran streaming out of my nostrils. I tried to tear at the stuff on my mouth, and couldn't. I was lying on my side and my hands were tied, very tightly, behind my back. My ankles were bound, too. I choked and heaved and thrashed around in the unspeakable agony of drowning in my own vomit.

'Get a basin and take that plaster off, before he chokes on his own sick!'

Hard fingernails scratched at my cheek, picking at the edge of the sticky tape. It was ripped off, and seemed to pull a layer of raw skin with it. Someone grabbed my hair and jerked my head over the side of what I learned later was a small iron cot. I was violently and painfully but also very gratefully sick into a

159

blue plastic washbasin placed under my face on the floor. When every last morsel of Sadie's roast-beef sandwiches was up and away, I lay back exhausted. My head was just one big bursting throb.

'Better now?'

I opened my eyes again and turned my face to look up. Someone huge bent over me, at least twice life-size. I blinked slowly until I was able to focus properly, and until he had stopped looming and receding like some blurred image in a surrealist movie. It was Chisholm. Smiling.

'We'll get you, you bastard . . .'

I said that because I was far too weary to think up anything smart. But it seemed to amuse him just the same. He threw back his head and laughed out loud.

'Oh, you poor mad buggers!' he said. 'You never know when you're whacked, do you?'

He had cut off a lot of his hair, and dyed the rest black. His skin had been lightly stained too. Gone was the fresh and freckled complexion. He now looked sallow, and had a network of lines on his face. They made it look thinner, and a lot older. Still, I should have recognised him. If he had not already been seated when I got to the cinema, if he had joined the granny after she had been seated herself, I probably would have.

'How did you get word to her?'

He shook his head mockingly. 'I didn't get

word to her, buddy. No one did.'

'You must have done.' I licked at the vile stuff caked around my lips. 'Because how else did she know exactly where to meet you? You were already there when she came in, and she went straight to the seat alongside of yours. I saw her.'

'You don't know very much about old ladies who play Bingo, do you, Farrow?' He laughed again. 'They get all sorts of funny ideas, you know. Like always using the same lucky pen, and always sitting in their own lucky place. My grandma has been sitting in that same seat for years, mate. The regulars keep it for her. All I had to do was be there early and make sure I got the one next to it. Simple, eh?'

While he was talking, I had been making a quick survey of the room. Big, almost square, about eighteen feet by twenty. Two single cots lay head to head along one wall and a third, the one I was on, at right angles to them against the other wall. There was a long dresser with a plate-rack top, and a square table with four hard chairs. In the corner opposite the door, next to the one big lace-curtained window, roomy cupboards had been built both under and above the thick pot sink. Two decent easy chairs flanked the old-fashioned coal fireplace and, diagonally across the corner beside it, a console television set. A man sat at the table,

161

eating. Chisholm saw me glance at him, and smiled.

'That's Dickie Petch. He thinks we ought to have killed you.'

The man looked up from his muttons, and nodded. 'Damned right,' he said, through a mouthful of something hot, 'and still do. So don't try to give us any trouble.'

He was a big one. Not young, but big. A two-inch belt of close-cropped greying hair ran over his ears and around the back of his strong square head, the rest of it was bald. He had hands like malt shovels and shoulders like a tough old bull. He chomped on his vittles as though he were eating braised railway spikes. Little gobs of whatever it was had fallen on to the front of his dark blue roll-neck sweater.

'That's good advice, Farrow.' Chisholm sat on the end of my cot. 'About not giving us any trouble, I mean. We're going on a long trip, and we're taking you with us. Keep your cool, and you'll be back in this land of hope of sod-all glory almost before you know you've been away. Try making any kind of fuss, and we'll dump you like a load of old ballast. You got that?'

'You'll never make it, Chisholm. You haven't a prayer.'

'Oh yes we will. So you might as well relax about it. Just keep thinking of the alternative.'

'Sure,' I said. I stopped straining my neck to look at him and let my face fall against the

162

covered pillow. I was talking now to the wallpaper. 'I'll think about what happened to Eldon. Did you give him the same sort of deal?'

Petch stopped eating and growled something in German, believing no doubt that I would not understand. He told Chisholm that he talked too much. Chisholm just laughed. He was just about as confident as ever they come.

'Oh, Eldon's all right,' he said. 'We just gave him a little fix. He never knew what hit him. He should be coming to'—he broke off slowly and I sensed rather than saw him looking at his watch—'around about now, I suppose. He won't feel so good, and it'll take him some time to get back on the road, but he'll make it all right. Old Dickie'—he laughed again—'wanted to kill him, too. He's a right bloodthirsty old bastard, isn't he?'

'And you're a bloody plaster saint,' I said. 'You just go around spreading sweetness and light. Is that it?'

'Well, I must admit that I do have my motives, Farrow. We did get you—it *was* you, wasn't it—out on the Oldham Road, didn't we? I know it didn't create a diversion big enough to let me see my granny without your interference, but it *did* work out all right in the end, didn't it? Come on now, be frank.'

'Who are you trying to impress, Chisholm?' What I really wanted to do was lie there quietly and marshal my resources against the pain, but

163

I had to keep him talking whilst he was still in the mood. 'Me, or your old pal Dickie? If it's me, I'd rather just be sick again.'

'I'm just telling you so you'll sleep easy, Farrow,' he went on. 'You've got a long wait, buddy. We're not leaving here until tomorrow. I wouldn't want you to spend the meantime racking your tiny pointed brain. I'm not a cruel man.'

'Why don't you face it, laddie. You're not any sort of man. You're just a stupid little shit who thinks he's on the side of the angels.'

Petch finished eating and got up to take his empty plate into the sink corner. I heard him rattling the pots around as he washed the dishes. When he was finished, he put his coat on.

'I'm going down to see if there's anything at the pick-up. Stay with him. All right?'

Chisholm laughed, and nudged me under the ear with my own Smith & Wesson. 'You hear that, Farrow? Dick's worried about us. He thinks you're going to jump up and burst your bonds and do me a mischief. You wouldn't be so nasty, would you?'

Petch's voice seemed to come from over by the door, as though he had paused there. 'Yes, well just don't get careless, that's all. This one's got more lives than a cat.'

He went out, and I asked Chisholm what about slackening off the ropes a little. He

164

chuckled, and said I really was a right bloody joker. I told him the ropes were cutting off the circulation and that if they wanted to get me to wherever it was they had in mind in anything like a decent state, he'd better do as I asked. He said all right then, but that I'd have to wait now until Dick came back. I hadn't honestly thought it would work, anyway. Instead, I tried to get him talking.

'Tell me something, Chisholm,' I said. 'Why Fylingdales? Where did it get you?'

'Where did it get us?' Chisholm laughed. He looked surprised. 'What the hell do you mean, where did it get us?'

'Don't tell me you did it just to show us how clever you are.'

'But of course, Farrow! What else? That's what the cold war is all about, buddy. An endless struggle to demonstrate in real terms that your Western notion of technical superiority is nothing more than a stupid, dangerous myth. "Anything you can do, we can do better. So don't go getting any funny ideas ..." That sort of thing.'

'What if it hadn't come off?'

'Christ! You still don't see, do you? It wouldn't greatly have mattered, friend. Except, of course, to the very few of us who were directly concerned. We'd have lost a battle, but not the war. Trouble with your lot, Farrow, is that you lack the facility to see yourselves against a background of history. Get the thing into perspective, boy. *We're* playing for *keeps!*'

Chisholm sat down, and I could see he was winding up to give me a long lesson in dialectics. Before he could get the bit between his teeth, I interrupted with a question somewhat closer to the heart.

'How's your dad these days?'

'My father was killed during the war, Farrow. He died, as they say, so that sods like you could live in a better world.'

'Is that a fact?' I said. 'Or could it be that when he died it wasn't really for real—I mean like that performance in Austria by your old lady?'

I had turned over on the cot to face the room. Chisholm was sitting at the table, the S&W in front of him. He smiled. 'Oh, yes,' he said, 'we heard all about your little trip to Kitzbuhel. You must think we're a lot of flaming amateurs, Farrow. But we're ahead of you, boy. We're ahead of you every time, all the time.'

'Yeah? Tell that to Jowysz.'

Chisholm scowled, and I knew I'd touched a sore spot. 'Jowysz died because his heart wasn't in the job,' he said. 'All that bloody nonsense about getting himself shrived. We should have known—once a mumbo-jumbo man, always a mumbo-jumbo man. He damn nearly got Petch caught, too. If you lot hadn't killed him, Petch would have saved you the trouble.'

166

'That I can believe. I suppose it was Petch took care of young Sutcliffe for you.'

'Petch and Jowysz, yes. But they didn't do it for *me*, Farrow. They did it for all of us. I was sorry it had to happen. Harold was a good mate of mine. I liked him, I really...'

'Yes?' I broke in. 'Well, you got a damn funny way of showing it. You did make the phone call that set him up for Petch, didn't you?'

'Shut up! Shut your bloody mouth or I'll put the tape back on!'

I had hurt him and he meant it and I didn't want my mouth taped up again, so I just shut up and set my face to the wall. Chisholm was still and quiet for a good ten minutes. Then I heard him get up, and the sounds of a kettle being filled. He set it on the gas ring in the sink corner, and there was the plop of lighted jets. More silence, then the small tea-making noises as he brewed up.

'Want a sup of tea, Farrow?'

'What are you trying to do'—I rolled over to face him—'kill me with kindness?'

'Oh, we're not going to kill *you* in any way, Farrow. Not 'less we have to, I mean.' He seemed to have regained his composure. 'No, not at all. You're our little bonus, matey. You should be good for a right nice swap.'

'Give over,' I said. 'They wouldn't swap me for a set of old cigarette cards. You're wasting your time.'

'Don't underrate yourself, buddy. We've done some good deals for blokes a lot less important than somebody from the Section. You're going to come in right useful, make no mistake about it.'

'You got anyone in mind?'

But Chisholm wasn't having any. He just didn't answer. He checked the teapot, and gave it a stir. Then he put two mugs on the table and asked me if I took milk and sugar. When he had poured it out, he helped me get up off the bed and on to a chair. I supped as much as I could by bending my head down to the mug and tilting it with my lips, then Chisholm held the mug up to my mouth while I drank the rest. The tea was strong and sweet and tasted good. I began to feel better, and hungry. I asked Chisholm when we were going to eat, and he said later. He got me back on to the bed and I let myself relax. I fell asleep. There may have been something in the tea.

I was roused by someone shaking my shoulder. Petch. There was a comforting smell of fish and chips. The kettle in the sink corner was steaming merrily, and the table was set with three plates. Chisholm was sitting at the table buttering slices of bread, from a cut loaf in a waxed wrapper. He grinned.

'Wake up, Farrow, it's feeding time. At least, it will be when we've had ours. You can watch us. Work yourself up an appetite.'

It was not necessary. Chisholm finished buttering the bread, and mashed the tea. Petch opened the black-leaded oven alongside the fireplace and took out a big newspaper-wrapped bundle of fish and chips. He separated two lots and put them, still in their inner wrapping of greaseproof paper, on to their plates. A couple of pieces of fish each, and a generous helping of chips. They salted and vinegared, and Chisholm ate with a knife and fork. Petch put his fish between slices of bread and ate the chips with his fingers. Either way would have done for me. I was starving.

When they were both finished, Chisholm came over to the bed. He slackened off a bit on the ropes around my hands. I sat there chafing my wrists and flexing my fingers. Petch got my fish and chips out of the oven and put them, paper and all, on the table. Then he poured out a mug of tea. My hands were swollen and so numb I could hardly hold the knife and fork. I ate slowly in spite of my hunger, trying to think up a plan of action. But it was hopeless. Petch sat on one of the beds behind my back with a big black automatic pistol in his fist, and Chisholm sat facing me across the table holding my own Smith and Wesson.

'Come on, Farrow, come on. Don't take all night over the job. If you don't want it, bloody well leave it.'

I put a spurt on, fearing that they might take the food away from me. I ate six slices of bread, every last scrap off the fish and chips paper, and drank two pots of tea. The tea was growing cold, but it went down well. When I was done, Chisholm bound my wrists, less tightly this time, and untied my ankles. Then he herded me out to a little windowless lavatory on the landing. Back on the bed, he tied my ankles yet again, and Petch told him to put tape on my mouth. Chisholm said what for, they were both going to be in, weren't they? Petch just grunted, and I started to breathe easy. He switched on the television set, and they slumped in the armchairs to watch the fifth showing of an old movie. I could not see the set except by making myself very uncomfortable, so lay back easy and settled for sound only. Every time I stirred, one of them got up to check that I wasn't doing a Houdini. Apart from that, it was quite a cosy evening.

After the movie, Chisholm made more tea, and I was taken again to the lavatory. My new suit was beginning to look decidedly aged. When they made me remove my jacket, I opted just to leave it off. Chisholm stuck a hypodermic needle into the rubber cap of a small bottle and drew off a measure of colourless liquid. He bent over the bed and pulled up my shirt sleeve.

'We're going to give you a little fix, Farrow.

Something to make you sleep sound, old buddy. So that *we* can kip without worrying about how you're getting on. Know what I mean?'

I felt the needle slide into my upper arm. He had made no attempt to sterilise the thing, and I remember hoping that I was not going to get an infection. That's the last thing I remembered. They must have used one of the opiate alkaloids, probably supplied by their chemist chum Jowysz. Soon I ceased to care about anything. I loved Chisholm like a brother, and I even felt drawn towards Petch. I slept.

THURSDAY

I woke up early and lay still for a while, listening to the muted sounds of traffic on a nearby road. Someone wearing clogs made iron music on the pavement below the window. The other two slept on, Petch on his back and snoring like an old boar. My head still ached, and felt like it was filled with kapok. After a while, I tried the ropes around my wrists. No good. Someone had taught Chisholm exactly how to do it. I was suffering badly from cramp, and did what I could to assist the circulation. My movements on the cot woke young

Chisholm, and he sat up quickly with the gun in his fist.

'Hold it, Farrow!'

I lay still while he got up and checked his knots. Satisfied, he sat back on his own bed and stretched and yawned. I watched him at his ablutions in the sink corner. Whilst he was dressing, Petch took his turn. His massive torso and thick arms were covered all over, back and front and shoulders, with curling grey hair. The way he looked, and especially the way I felt, he could have eaten me before breakfast.

I had a pressing need of nature, and was wondering whether to try to wait until I was strong enough perhaps to turn the opportunity to some sort of advantage. I decided not, and told Chisholm that I had to go. He untied my ankles, and I told him that this time I was going to need my hands, too. Chisholm hesitated. Petch stopped towelling himself and crossed to his bed. He put a hand beneath the pillow and came up with his .45. He jerked on the slide to put one up the spout, and nodded.

'All right, let him go.'

They made me leave the door open. Chisholm stood on the landing watching me at my private function, and Petch lounged in the doorway with his big black pistol. He kept it pointed, almost negligently, right at the most vulnerable parts of my person. I sat there miserably, eyeing the closed door at the bottom of the stairs and very conscious of the trousers draped around my ankles. The calculation of my chances needed no computer. I would not even get to my feet. Petch looked as though he was actually hoping I might make the effort. Chisholm was just embarrassed.

When I was all through they let me have a wash, but not a shave, at the sink. I managed, while rinsing myself at the running tap, to drink a lot of water. There was a small mirror. My face looked even worse than before, but actually felt much better. The cut under my eye seemed to be knitting well, and the one in my scalp was scabbing over nicely. My flagged spirits began to rise.

'Come on, Farrow, stop admiring your bloody self and get into them.'

'Them' were a navy blue roll-neck sweater, twin to the one worn by Petch and bearing down the front his trade mark of spilled food, a much-used boiler suit which smelled very much of fish, and a worn pair of Wellingtons. The clothes fitted more or less all right, but the Wellingtons were a couple of sizes too big.

'The Wellingtons are too big.'

'Aw, sod it!' Chisholm made a parody of acute dismay. 'Does that mean you won't be able to come with us? Hear that, Dickie?' He winked at Petch, who was sitting on his coat and holding the .45 on me, 'Farrow doesn't like you 'cos your feet's too big!'

'Come on, come on.' Petch just wasn't in the

mood. He looked as though the early morning was not his best time. Him and Charlie would have made a good pair. 'Stop the skylarking and get on with some breakfast. We haven't got all day.'

Chisholm got the frying pan cracking, and I must say he would have made a pretty good short-order cook. They had sausages and bacon and two eggs and fried bread, then watched me eat the same. Afterwards, I felt a lot better. But not for long. Chisholm did his little act with the hypodermic, and my plans for breaking loose seemed suddenly unimportant. I judged from the effects that they must have switched this time to one of the drugs in the datura group, possibly scopolamine. I began almost at once to have trouble remembering who I was, and what it was all about. They sat me on the bed, and I slumped there with my back against the wall, struggling ineffectively with every atom of mental energy I could muster against an overpowering lethargy and acquiescence.

I watched dully as they made their preparations for leaving. The details escaped me then, and still do. How long it took them, I do not know. It could have been as much as a couple of hours. They herded me down the stairs, through a room on the ground floor, and out of a door leading into a big closed outhouse with a corrugated-iron roof. The room on the ground floor was a fish and chip shop, the big pans still and cold. The outhouse had a concrete floor and I remember galvanised iron wash-tubs filled to the top with water and peeled potatoes. A long wooden trough running down most of one wall was packed with crushed ice and great, staring cod. The place had big double doors, and parked inside was a battered grey Bedford van. Petch leaned me against an ugly drum-like iron potato peeler, and unlocked the truck doors. They made me lie down inside on fish-smelling sacks and Chisholm climbed in beside me with the Smith & Wesson. I was aware of the noise as Petch started the motor. He got out then to open up the outhouse doors, and Chisholm held the S&W hard against my left ear as he backed the van into the street. Then we were away.

I lay there quietly with my eyes closed, and raged inwardly against the desire to sleep and forget. My heart pounded massively and I used its heavy beating as a sort of metronome to help me repeat, over and over again, the basic facts of my identity and situation. The truck jolted on, mile after mile and what seemed like hour after hour. I stuck desperately to my single purpose, fighting the drug with all I had and sweating so much inside the boiler suit that I could feel it run off my ribs in streams. There was no pain now, only an overwhelming distress. I bit my lips to stifle any mumblings and prayed, when I could think of it, that

175

Chisholm would suppose I was asleep. I thought between times of Charlie, and what *he* would do. It helped a lot.

After a long time we stopped. I was so tired I could hardly bring myself to take notice. But I felt Chisholm tense, and opened my eyes to see the snub barrel of the S&W not six inches from the end of my nose. I heard the cab door slam as Petch got out. He was gone, so far as I could judge, about five minutes. When he returned, and we had set off again, I went back to my exercises. Soon afterwards, we stopped again. Chisholm nudged me, not gently, with the Smith & Wesson.

'Come on, tiger. Upsadaisy...'

He got me sitting upright and I slumped there like a puppet with its strings cut. We waited. I made as though to lie down again. Chisholm slapped me sharply, and stuck the pistol hard against my Adam's apple. Soon, the rear doors were flung open and Petch was helping.

'Come on, move him!'

The van was parked hard against the kerb in a narrow street flanked on our side by a very high wall of purple brick. Backed up close to us was a black Vauxhall car with a sign on its roof which said TAXI. The rear door on the pavement side was thrown wide open. Petch grabbed my ankles and heaved. One of my Wellingtons came off in his hand. He cursed viciously and jammed it back on again. There was another man with him, a squat, nervous character with a hare lip. This one hopped around whilst Petch and Chisholm dragged and pushed to get me out of the van, talking a blue hysterical streak and every second word beginning with *f*. Petch told him angrily to shut up and get himself back into the cab. It seemed to take them an hour to get me out of the van and into the back seat of the taxi. It probably took all of one full minute. Chisholm got in with me, and I felt the muzzle of his gun press hard into my ribs. Petch slammed the door shut, and told the driver to get on his way. A lorry passed, but did not slow down. Our driver waited until it had drawn well away from us, then followed in the same direction.

I felt very much, and must have looked and acted, like a sick sad drunk. But I clung grimly to my orientation routine and contrived at intervals to swing my lolling head around and snatch glimpses of the passing scene. It took a lot longer than it should have but I succeeded, even before we hit the docks, in placing our whereabouts. We were in Hull. We had run out along Hedon Road in the direction of the King George dock, passed the prison and maternity hospital, and turned left. Ten minutes later we were passing the prison again. Chisholm noticed it, too. He leaned across the back seat beside the driver's, scowling.

'Here, what the hell's going on? We've been down this way once already!'

Hare-lip glanced up into the mirror and nodded. He looked worried. 'Keep your effing shirt on, lad,' he said. 'The effing pubs have only just effing well closed, haven't they? We don't want to be the only effing taxi on the effing dock, do we? Any minute now there'll be dozens of the effers. See what I mean?'

Chisholm did see what he meant and so, I was vaguely pleased to note, did I. They were going to put me on board a ship. *Brilliant, Marcus. Take it from there.* Yes, well ... a real old genuine Bedouin of a Kingston-upon-Hull taxi, probably quite well known at the docks, bringing a couple of drunken deck-hands back to their floating home. Nothing extraordinary about that. It was in fact so damned *perfectly* ordinary that it could not fail to work.

And it didn't. Our driver slowed down in Corporation Road to let another taxi overtake him, and followed the cab through the dock gates. Close, but not too close. He did not even have to stop. The man on the gate just waved, and hare-lip waved back. Chisholm breathed a great sigh of relief, and sank back beside me on the upholstery. If I had been just a little stronger, a little less dopey, I might have tried it. As it was, my thinking was still very muzzy, and I felt like a piece of chewed string, but I was not that stupid. I wasn't even strong

178

enough to shout. All it might have got me would be another gash on the head.

We bumped along the cobbled dock between great stacks of timber on the one side and a line of moored ships on the other. Chisholm leaned forward to say something to the driver, and he drew in close to the gangplank of a rust-streaked freighter. He was out of the driving seat in a flash and had the rear door open. Chisholm got out, then leaned back in to haul me out too. Nobody anywhere ever looked, or felt, more drunk. My legs would not support my reeling body, and they had to place themselves one on either side of me with my arms across their shoulders. The freighter, a Russian timber ship of around fifteen hundred tons, had discharged her cargo and was riding high out of the water. The gangplank seemed steep as Everest, and would not keep still. The little cab driver was effing and blinding twenty to the dozen and Chisholm, who was supporting most of my fourteen stone, was gasping hoarsely like a sow in pig. But other willing hands came quickly to their assistance, and I was dragged bodily over the scuppers. They propped me, swaying, against the deckhouse bulkhead.

The two seamen who held me upright whilst Chisholm passed a bundle of notes to the taxi driver eyed me curiously but kept their mouths shut. I sagged against them, pretending to be worse off than I was. Chisholm said something, and they hustled me forward along the starboard side and through a hatch in the boat-deck casing. My feet slipped on the worn metal steps, and I clutched the handrail to stop myself hurtling headlong down the ladder. One of the seamen grabbed at the collar of my boiler suit, and I managed with his help to hit the deck below still on my feet. Then Chisholm took over, and the seaman hurried forrard along the narrow companionway to open up a small hatch to a compartment under the forepeak. Chisholm shoved me through, and came in after me. The seaman stood just outside the hatch, waiting. Now, he had a gun in his hand.

We were in a V-shaped compartment on the mess deck, right up in the bows. There was a single deadlight in the deckhead, and some little daylight from two small anchor ports. The Russians were using the place as a paint locker, and for the stowage also of hard stores. There wasn't much room. Chisholm pushed me down on my backside with my shoulders against a coil of three-inch rope. He knelt in front of me with his knees astride my legs, fumbled in the pocket of his windbreaker jacket, and took out a two-ounce tobacco tin and a small penknife. I watched him with what I hoped was apparently a lot less interest than I actually felt.

He used the penknife to make a four-inch slit right through all three of my sleeves—a boiler suit, jersey, and shirt—then opened up his tobacco tin. When I saw what was inside, I knew he wasn't just going to roll me a tickler. The syringe was in two parts, barrel and needle. He fitted them together, then filled the thing with what was left in his bottle. Carefully, he held the syringe up to the light and squeezed the plunger to expel any air. Clear fluid spurted briefly from the end of the needle, and he leaned forward to take my arm.

'Come on, Farrow, my old mate. One last little fix, eh? That's the way, easy now . . .'

I waited until he'd got the needle right in and had started to press down on the plunger. Then I jerked away. The needle snapped and Chisholm cursed and I felt the gush of wetness as the drug ran down my bared arm. Chisholm sat back suddenly on his heels, his face gone red with rage. He flung the empty hypodermic past my left shoulder, and I heard it smash against the bulkhead. Then he came at me with the penknife, and I thought he was going to let me have it. But he just grabbed at the end of rope and started sawing at it. I might have got him then, but there was only one way out, and the man who was blocking it looked as though he knew very well how to use the thing he had in his hand. Chisholm finished sawing through the rope, and began to separate the three main strands.

'All right, tiger. You asked for it. So we'll do

it the hard way. We're cleared for Customs, but there's nearly three hours to wait for the tide. Then we've another two hours in the estuary, with the pilot on board. That's five hours you're going to be trussed up, chum, and I hope you enjoy every bloody one of them!'

All the time he talked he was working on my wrists and ankles. I tried to brace my hands and make my wrists big, but he wasn't having any. He pulled the rope cruelly tight. When he was done, he said something in Russian to the seaman, who dragged off the grubby sweat rag looped around his neck. Chisholm turned me over and pulled the thing between my teeth. It tasted like old socks. He knotted the ends behind my neck then sat back on his heels, breathing heavily, to review his handiwork. He nodded, and wiped perspiration off his brow with the back of his wrist.

'That should hold you, matey. Maybe next time you'll do yourself a favour. Settle for the easy way.'

He stood over me, stooping slightly under the deckhead. Then he turned away. The hatch clanged shut and I heard the clips slam home. Someone dropped something heavy on to the deck above my head, and there was a muffled rumble of Russian gutturals. The ship heaved ever so gently, and somewhere near my left ear a fender rubbed against the dock. Out in the river, a ship's horn sounded two long melancholy blasts. *You and me both, chum*, I thought. *You and me both*. I closed my eyes and lay there on my side and willed myself to relax. Before too long, I began properly to *think*. It felt great. The facility seemed to feed upon itself, and pretty soon I was figuring things out along with the best of them.

Once the ship was clear of the Humber and outside of territorial waters they could lash me to the bows and use me for a figurehead, but until then I was definitely *persona non grata*. Chisholm would certainly check on me just before the pilot came on board, and probably once or twice again during the time we were in the estuary. In the meantime I had to get loose, and the sooner the better. The ropes binding my wrists were pulled too tight for me to wriggle out of. They would have to be cut. What I needed was a rough edge on something. An angle-iron, serrated by the acetylene torch and left untrimmed. Anything.

My first thought was of the casing around the hatch, and I wasted a lot of time on it. I caterpillared across, levered myself upright against the bulkhead, and began sawing away. But the rim of the weld had been rubbed smooth, and all my efforts got me was a massive ache across the shoulders, and wrists chafed nearly raw. Twice I heard footsteps in the gangway outside, and twice I bruised myself hitting the deck and wriggling back desperately to resume the position in which Chisholm had left me. When it happened the third time, and I was no further forward, I gave it up and looked around for something else.

Which is what I should have done in the first place. The coil of rope from which Chisholm had cut the length to tie me up was resting against a bale of cleaning rags—and the bale was bound with thin flat metal straps about half an inch wide. The top of the bale had been slashed open, and some of the rags pulled out. Some, but not nearly enough. The bale was still too full, and the rags too tightly packed, for there to be sufficient play on the binding for my purpose. I had to get more out of one end of the bale in order to win some slack. I got to my knees beside the bale, and by the use of muscles I didn't even know I had, went into an act which would not have disgraced your average contortionist.

The rags had been packed under pressure, and hauling them out was murder. I was getting a lot of pain now from the broken needle lodged in my arm. The tiny piece sticking out kept snagging on the cut sleeves. I was forced to take frequent rests. My body was bathed in sweat but my feet, because Chisholm had pulled off the Wellingtons before he tied my ankles, felt cold. I tugged and twisted in that impossible position for what seemed like hours. Each time I wrestled out a complete piece of rag, I edged sixty painful sideways inches on my aching knees to drop it out of sight behind a low pyramid of two-inch boiler pipe stacked against the starboard bulkhead. After a long time I was able to tug the rags out of the bale with much less effort, and I judged there to be enough slack in one of the metal strips for me to get a wrist on either side of it. I dragged out one last piece of somebody's old vest and lay down, gasping, for a long breather.

I was still resting when Chisholm came back. I heard the clips being slapped off the hatch, and his low chuckle as he stepped over the coaming. He knelt by my side, and I pretended to have been asleep. When he rolled me over to check on his handiwork I groaned out loud, and it was no act. He heaved me back on to my side.

'That's a boy, Farrow. Not long now, you sad old bastard. Pilot's on his way, and we should be casting off in about five minutes. I hope you're a good sailor. There's a force-nine gale warning, and this old tub's going to roll like buggery...'

He moved away from me and sat on the deck with his back to a big round drum of what looked from the drippings like red lead. I thought for one sick moment that he was going to stay in the forepeak until we dropped the pilot. Almost as though he were reading my thoughts, he chuckled.

'Don't let me keep you off your beauty sleep,

old buddy,' he said. 'Soon as the pilot is settled on the bridge, I'm going down aft to eat. You'll just have to wait. We'll feed you later—if you're good, that is...'

He went rabbiting on about how much we were both going to enjoy our little holiday. I lay there quite still with my eyes closed, listening to the special sounds a ship makes as it prepares to leave harbour. The barely perceptible deepening of the engine note, and a sudden quickening of all movement. Nothing very much you can put your finger on, but by experience and association, the sensations are unmistakable. I caught the authoritative note of command in a voice raised above decks, and sensed rather that felt the ship's subtle motion as she slipped away from the side of the dock. A few minutes later, Chisholm got to his feet. He seemed to be in a state of rare elation, as though he were sure now that his troubles were already over.

'Well, Farrow, we're on our way. Be good, and I'll see you later.'

Soon as he was gone, I got on with it. The going was tougher, even, than I had imagined. I couldn't begin to work on the ropes until I had thought of a way to brace the flexible steel slat in a rigid position. And that, in my condition, took some little time. Finally, I had it figured out. All I had to do then was put the plan in operation. By the time I was ready to start on the ropes I felt black and blue all over and was forced to take another long rest.

Chisholm had switched off the deadlight on leaving me that last time, and by now it was nearly dark. But I was working almost entirely by touch, anyway. I found a three-foot length of piping among the pieces stacked against the bulkhead, and got one end of it wedged firmly between the metal strap and the rags left jammed in the bale. Next time you happen to have your hands tied behind your back, you should try it. Then, by bracing the pipe against my side, I was able to keep the strap taut and firm and edge-on to my fumbling wrists. The pipe kept slipping, and it was a tortuous business. The strain was killing, but I could actually feel the sharp rusty strap sawing through the strands. Haste made me fumble, and I could feel it sawing at my wrists, too. By the time I finally broke free the sides of my fists were lacerated badly and running with blood.

First thing I did when my hands fell apart was tear at the filthy gag and pull it down under my chin. Then I let myself sag against the bale, drawing great gulps of air in through my mouth. My clothes were soaked in sweat, and I felt completely dehydrated. Right then, I would have given anything I possessed for just one long pull at a pint of ale.

Suddenly, I was cold. When I bent forward at last to tug at the knots in the rope around my ankles, the wet clothes felt chill and clammy against my spine. I freed my feet, then leaned back against the bale to pick at the needle stuck in my arm. My thumb and fingernails kept slipping off the tiny end protruding from the skin, but eventually I got the thing out. Somehow, it made me feel better. I groped around for the Wellingtons, and drew them on. Just having something on my feet made me feel a lot less vulnerable too. I began to massage my much-abused limbs, and not to be trussed up was marvellous. After only a very little while, I began to think real good.

I switched on the deadlight, and chose myself a full five-gallon drum. I set it down on the deck beside the bale of rags, raised my trusty pipe in both hands, and brought the end down sharply on the lid near the rim. The lid buckled inwards with not too much of a thump, and black paint spurted out. I jumped quickly to the bulkhead and flattened myself beside the hatch in case the noise had been heard in the mess deck, but minutes passed and nobody came. So I laid down my length of piping and set about preparing a little diversion. I dragged more rags out of the bale, tilting the drum with one hand to slop paint all over them. Soon, I had a good big pile, all nicely soaked and ready. I took off my well-splashed boiler suit and threw that on top. Then I sat on the deck beside the hatch with the length of pipe across my knees, waiting for Chisholm.

He did not show for a long time, and I began to be afraid he would not return until after the pilot was dropped. I strained my ears to listen for any slowing-down of the engine beat, or any other sound which might indicate the coming alongside of the pilot launch. I had to make my play before he was off the ship. Once he was clear, my chances of success would be greatly reduced. Still Chisholm did not come. I clambered over a stack of paint drums and knelt gingerly on a heap of rusted chain to peer through the starboard anchor port. The many lights of Grimsby were almost directly opposite, and Spurn Head must be coming up on the port bow. It had to be now. I actually had my hand on the first of the hatch clips when I heard his footsteps in the gangway.

I reached up quickly and switched off the deadlight, then flattened against the bulkhead just aft of the hatch with the length of piping all ready raised in my right hand. The clips dropped away one by one, and he swung the hatch wide open. There was some light from the gangway, but he could not see that I was no longer where he'd left me until he stepped over the coaming. As he did so, I let him have it. I was in no condition to keep my end up in any kind of brawl, and too uncertain of my remaining strength to make any valid judgement of force. So I just took a half swing and hit him hard as I could. He pitched forward flat on his face, and I dropped on him quickly with my knees in his back. I had the pipe raised for another belt, but it was not necessary. There was no sign of a split in his skull, but he was knocked out cold.

First thing I did was roll him over and feel for my Smith & Wesson. With that in my fist, they could *all* bloodywell come. The dimly lit gangway was deserted, but the hatch just forrard of the ladder was latched open, and I could hear voices. I pussy-footed up to it, with the length of piping in one hand and the Smith & Wesson in the other, and looked in. At first, I saw only three of them. Then I noticed another one, turned in snug and asleep on his bunk. Two of the ones still up were playing a game of cards on the mess table, and the other guy was reading. None of them glanced up. I moved over to stand square in front of the open hatch and stepped over the coaming.

They saw me then, all right. The one who was reading dropped his book with a stifled curse and made to lunge to his feet. One of the card players, an older man, uttered a sharp instruction and put a hand on his arm to hold him down. I nodded, and stepped to one side of the hatch with my back against the bulkhead.

'That's the style, Grandpa. Keep 'em cool. I don't know if you buggers speak any English, and I don't much care. But this is the way of it.

Stay below and mind your own business and none of you need get hurt. Try to interfere, and I swear to God I'll kill as many of you as I can. You got that?'

The old man said something. I don't know if he was translating, or just guessing. The others stared at me, and whichever way it was I could tell they were getting the message. All the time, I was glancing around. There was only this one hatch into the mess deck, and the scuttles in the outer bulkhead were too small even for anyone to get his head through. The old man finished his little chat, and fell silent. I nodded again.

'That's right. Just all of you sit here quietly and keep your bloody mouths shut.'

I backed out and closed the hatch with my shoulder. The gangway was still deserted. I swung the clips on and then, fitting my length of pipe over the ends of each one, used it as a lever to tighten them hard. Without a heavy hammer, or something of the same sort to use on the other side, they were well and truly confined to quarters. This done, I sped back to the forepeak for a quick check on Chisholm. He was lying exactly how I'd left him, breathing in shallow gasps. There would be no danger from him for some time to come.

I made it unchallenged to the top of the ladder, and stepped out on to the upper deck. The clean night air hit me like a friendly little slap in the face. I stood there, flattened against the winch room bulkhead, and drank it in. Just to feel free and unfettered worked wonders for my bludgeoned spirit, and the length of piping seemed suddenly superfluous. I dropped it over the side. It was quite dark now, the only illumination coming from the riding lights. I nipped across the beam via the thwart-ships gangway behind and below the boat deck, and stole up the ladder on the port side. The wireless cabin was directly aft of the wheelhouse, and a glow from its open hatch cast a short pale swath of light on the water sliding past the ship's side. I edged up to it and peeped in.

There was a bunk in the cabin, and the radio operator lay on top of it. He was immersed in a magazine. The pictures, from what I could see of them, were pretty riveting. I'd always thought the Russians did not permit that sort of stuff. Maybe he bought it in Hull. I watched him turn the page.

'Pssst . . .' I said.

He lowered the magazine, saw me standing there with the gun on him, and sat bolt upright. He opened his mouth. I held a finger to my lips and cocked the Smith & Wesson and he closed it again. I stepped inside, up to the bunk. The banks of wireless equipment were humming softly and giving off the usual spasmodic crackle of unintelligible mush. Still with my finger to my lips, I motioned with the pistol for him to roll over on to his face. He did so, and I slugged him behind the ear. He stiffened momentarily, let out just one tiny gasp, and then flopped down limp. I straddled the stool in front of the R/T set, and switched to Transmit. By this time, my hands were definitely trembling. I spun the right knobs most of the time, but it took me longer than it should have to find the correct frequency. I started to send out a Mayday. My fingers shook so much on the knob that it must have gone across very much like the real thing. The nerves in my back crawled and jumped with the expectation at any time of a heavy blow. I swung half-round, still transmitting with my left hand, so that I could cover the door.

That was when I saw the Very gun. It lay on its rack, just inside the hatch. Beneath it, secure in their spring clips, a neat row of six giant cartridges. I stopped transmitting, and used some recently acquired skills to put the radio gear very firmly out of action. They would not repair that lot in much less than twenty-four hours. This done, I lifted the signal pistol off its rack and pulled at the big fat shells clipped beneath it. I broke the pistol, slid a shell into the breech, and stuffed a couple of spares into my trousers pockets. Behind me, the wireless operator groaned piteously and tried to turn over. I threw him one last look, tucked the Smith & Wesson firmly into my waistband, and stepped out on to the boat deck with the loaded signal pistol held down by my side. I could hear some talk from the wheelhouse just forrard, and it sounded like English. Out on the river, off the port beam, the lights of the oncoming pilot launch bobbed and swayed on the light swell. It was all happening.

I hurried down the ladder on to the main deck and crossed the thwart-ships gangway. As I turned aft to make for the hatch down to the mess deck, a shadowy figure moved out from behind the winch room and spoke to me in Russian. It sounded like a question. I grunted something unintelligible, and pushed past him. As I did so, he caught sight of my face in the light from an open scuttle. He grabbed at my arm and I swung round fast and laid the heavy barrel of the Very pistol hard against the side of his head. He fell against the bulkhead and dropped to his knees. I stooped over to let go with another one, but he slumped sideways, unconscious, before I could hit him again.

I ran down the ladder and past the still-clamped mess-deck hatch. Nobody tried to stop me. Chisholm was still lying where I left him, but he was groaning now and trying to push himself up off the deck. I put the Very pistol on top of the red lead drum and bent down to grab him under the armpits. He struggled weakly, but I hauled him to the hatch and dragged him over the coaming into the gangway. He was beginning to come round, but wouldn't be any sort of real threat for quite a while. I ducked back into the paint locker and fired a round from the Very pistol into my heap of paint-soaked rags.

The blast from the Very in that confined space sounded like the firing of a fair-sized missile. The big blazing cartridge smacked into the rags, and the small compartment was filled instantly with searing glare and heat. I backed out smartly, and reloaded with feverish haste. Chisholm was on his feet, swaying crazily and tottering from one side of the narrow gangway to the other. I came up running and shoved him heavily in front of me to the ladder. The men in the mess deck were battering frenziedly at the hatch, and I could hear them yelling for help. I ignored them and half lifted, half pushed the mumbling Chisholm up the ladder ahead of me.

Soon as I'd got him out in the open I pointed the Very at the moon and pulled the trigger. There was a terrific bang, and the bright red flare soared up through the night sky in a lovely flaming parabola. It seemed to hang for an instant at the top of its arc, then burst brilliantly into several separate stars, each one looking brighter than the rest. I broke open the breech, slid in my last cartridge, and loosed off again. The flares hung over us for several long seconds, bathing the ship in a light far brighter than day. I heard a shout of alarm, and looked up to see someone on the flying bridge. Probably the skipper. He started to yell, and I heard feet pounding along the deck somewhere aft. I flung the signal pistol over the side.

Chisholm was coming round. I had been leaning hard into him, pinning him with my weight against the low rail. Now, I stooped quickly, grabbed him just below the knees, and heaved. He toppled overboard with a hoarse cry, hit the water with a tremendous splash, and sank like a stone. I marked the place where he'd gone down, and climbed over the rail. Someone rushed up and made a grab at me. I pushed him off with a hand in the face, and jumped.

The water closed over me with a jarring shock. It was bitterly cold. I struggled desperately to the surface and trod water, looking for Chisholm. I spotted his head about twenty feet away. He was threshing around weakly, gulping and gasping and coughing up streams of dirty Humber water. It looked as though he could not swim. I struck out towards him, and got a hold on his collar. One of his arms came round like a flail and the clenched fist caught me high on the cheek-bone. The one that was cut already. I felt one of the stitches go, and the pain brought tears to my eyes. I grabbed for Chisholm's head, found a fistful of hair, and forced him under. When he came up, choking and spluttering, I put my face close to his and yelled at the top of my lungs.

'Keep still, you little bastard, or I'll bloody well let you drown!'

I got him on his back, hooked an arm under his chin, and struck out away from the ship. Smoke and flames were shooting out of the anchor ports, and the upper decks seemed filled with scurrying figures silhouetted against the glare. The pilot boat was approaching on the other side, and I swam away from it. All I wanted the pilot boat to do was to take the pilot off. Unless I was very much mistaken, the Spurn Head lifeboat would be with us in just about no time at all. Good old Spurn Head, the only lifeboat station in the whole of Great Britain with a permanent, full-time crew. *So come on then, lads, it's very damned cold in here!*

Chisholm lay quietly on the water now, and I was able to keep him afloat without too much trouble. The timber ship was carrying a lot of light, though the anchor ports were belching nothing now but thick black smoke. It probably looked a lot worse than it was. I paddled us both around to face the north shore, and caught my first glimpse of the lifeboat. I could see from her lights that she was bows-on to us at about a mile and a half, and bearing down fast. I towed Chisholm into what I judged to be a collision course, and just stroked away easy to keep our heads afloat. Soon as the boat hove into hailing distance I waved my free arm and hollered for all I was worth. I could have saved my breath. The lookout had seen us already.

The bows swung in over us and I made a grab with my free hand at one of the lifelines looping down from the gunwales. I hooked my arm over it and hugged Chisholm in close to my chest. Hands reached down to help. They hauled us inboard like sacks of wet sawdust, and we slumped there gasping and choking like landed fish. One of the crew threw blankets around us. The boat lurched as the cox'n opened the throttle, and hove round to head again for the timber ship. There wasn't even much smoke now, and I guessed that the crew had brought my fire under control.

'You off the Russki?' One of the crewmen handed me a bottle and I took a long pull. The rum spread out along my bones like liquid heat. I took another pull, handed the bottle to Chisholm, and shook my head. 'No, no. Bugger all to do with us—except that she ran us down, I mean. Our own fault, mind. We saw her, all right. I just thought we were going to make it across her bows. We didn't, and that's all there is to it.'

Chisholm was slumped on the thwarts beside me, the picture of abject defeat. He said nothing. I reached the bottle out of his limp hand, took another swig, then handed it over. Before putting the cap back on, the crewman gave himself another little sup. Just, I supposed, to keep us company.

'Didn't the pilot see you?' he persisted. 'Weren't you carrying any lights? What were you in?'

'Oh, the old boat's not much of a loss,' I said. 'I'm just bloody glad we didn't go down with it. Young Fred here can't even swim...'

It wasn't a very convincing story, but there was no time right then for anyone to question it. We were coming alongside the timber ship. The rusty bulk of her loomed above us, rising and falling on the light swell. The crewman who had been asking the questions jumped away to help fend us off, and I looked up to see dark figures leaning over the rail. One of them was yelling something in English, and I guessed he must be the pilot. The cox'n made a funnel of his hands.

'That you, Harry? What the hell's going on?'

'Fire in the paint locker!' The pilot sounded puzzled, and I could not say I blamed him. 'Skipper says they've got it under control now, though, so it looks like a false alarm so far as you lads are concerned. What took you so long?'

The cox'n laughed. 'Get knotted!' he yelled. It had taken the lifeboat all of six minutes to launch and get out there. 'What about the bloody boat you ran down? You goin' blind in your old age, or what?'

'What boat? We've hit no boat. What the hell

you on about?'

The rum was wearing off and I started to shiver. I could hear Chisholm's teeth chattering and he sagged against me, huddled down in his blanket and not caring now about any of it. I bet he had one hell of a headache. The Russian skipper assured the pilot that all of his crew were accounted for, and that everything was now under control. What else could he say? He was probably glad to be shot of the whole damned business. All he wanted now was to square himself with the lifeboat crew, drop the pilot, and get on his merry way.

I pulled at the sleeve of the crewman who had given us the rum. 'Here, mate,' I said. 'What about putting us ashore before we get double pneumonia?'

But the cox'n was insisting that there would need to be an inquiry. He wanted the Russian to put back into Hull. The skipper said no, and he wasn't going to put into Grimsby, either. There was a lot of heated exchange. The skipper swore that he was due in Hull with another cargo just five weeks hence, and said he would attend any amount of inquiries then. The pilot confirmed his story, and sided with him. Finally, and much to my relief, it was agreed that the ship should continue on course. The pilot transferred to his launch, and his mate brought the little boat around and across the freighter's bows. We pushed off ourselves, and the lifeboat's heavy engine rumbled throatily as the cox'n opened her up. I heard the clang of his engine-room bell as the Russian skipper signalled for half ahead, and the water under his stern churned up dirty white.

Quite suddenly there was another kind of noise, and we all looked up. As we did, the lifeboat was bathed in hard white light, and we covered our eyes against the glare. The big helicopter whoppered in so low it seemed about to settle on our heads, and the down-draught from the whirling blades beat atop of us and flattened the water all around the boat into a black maelstrom of tiny ripples. Somebody leaned so perilously far out of the open door that I was sure he must fall.

I knew it was Charlie even before I got a look at his mug. I stood up in the thwarts and let the blanket drop off my shoulders. He waved, and I thought for a second that I saw a smile on his face. It was probably just a trick of the light. I saw his mouth moving, but the noise and the wind flung his yell back into his teeth. I pointed at Chisholm, still slumped disconsolately in his blanket, then at the lights of Spurn Head. Charlie nodded violently, got back into his seat, and the helicopter rose noisily. The pilot cut the searchlight and banked off sharply, tilting sideways and upwards, and soared away. Every man in the lifeboat crew watched this little pantomime with mouths agape. The cox'n made

201

his way to my side.

'What's all this then? What's going on?'

Chisholm looked up at that, and I felt under my blanket for the gun. Miraculously, I still had it, and that made me feel almost warm again. Not because I thought I might need that kind of help so far as Chisholm was concerned. I just hated the thought of having to tell Charlie I'd lost it. But I gave Chisholm a nudge with the muzzle anyway, in case he might still be harbouring any foolish ideas.

'Look,' I told the cox'n, 'all I can tell you is that this is not a thing for you boys to worry over. I'm sure somebody will tell you all about it some time, but it won't be me and it's not going to be now.' Then to ward off any further questions, I asked one of my own. 'How long back to Spurn Head—can you speed us up a bit?'

The cox'n, thank God, was an intelligent man. He just nodded, and went back aft to the wheel. I felt the big boat shudder, and the stumpy bows rose as he gave her the gun. Almost at once, it seemed, he was throttling down to ease her up to the concrete slipway at Spurn Head. Charlie and two other men were waiting on the ramp to grab the gunwales and help draw the boat alongside.

'Farrow—you all right?'

''Course I'm all right.' I waved the hand away and climbed up on to the jetty under my own steam. 'I always go in for a swim around this time. Look what I found in the river.'

Chisholm looked up at us from the thwarts, his eyes dull and lifeless. A couple of crewmen boosted him up, and we got him out on to the dock. Charles looked at him, and nodded.

'Bloody good show. Come on, let's get him back to the whirlybird.'

'Here, hang on a minute, Charlie,' I said. 'That hogwash was very damned wet, you know! It was cold, too. That's not castanets you're hearing, old lad, it's my bloody teeth chattering. You may have noticed that I've got no sodding shoes on, either...'

Charlie glanced down at my feet, then turned to one of the fascinated lifeboat men. 'You got any dry gear in the station?'

The man nodded and we all trooped up the ramp, Chisholm and I clutched in our blankets and dripping a trail of dirty water. First thing we saw in the lifeboat station crew-room was the big roaring stove. We stripped off mother-naked in front of it, and rubbed ourselves dry. The cox'n dug out some clothes for us. Ex W/D trousers, rough flannel shirts, thick socks, and roll-neck sweaters. He said he was sorry there was no underwear and I told him that was all right. The clothes were a fair fit, but the boots were tight. Who cared. I had hidden the Smith & Wesson in the folds of my wet slacks and now I retrieved it. All this time,

203

Chisholm had not uttered a single word. Charlie had the cox'n in a corner and was telling him some kind of story. I could see the lifeboat man nodding. One of the men who had come with Charlie was standing by the door. The other one, who I supposed was the helicopter pilot, had disappeared. Chisholm had finished dressing and was slumped on a seat just staring at the stove. I wondered what he was thinking.

Outside, I felt cold again. The man with Charlie caught hold of Chisholm's forearm, and I heard a metallic click as he snapped a cuff on him. He locked its mate on to his wrist, and we were away. The narrow spit of land running out to Spurn Head is just about wide enough to take the road, and the helicopter man had put his machine down right in the middle of it. The hulking bird loomed up at us out of the darkness, its rotor blades drooping sadly just over our heads. The pilot was sitting in at the controls, hands clamped over his headphones and talking quietly into a throat mike. As we came up, he leaned forward to flick off a switch, and grinned down at us. Before, in the dark, I had not recognised him. Now, in the faint light of his instrument panel, I did. It was Sam Harvey.

'Well, bugger me!' I said. 'If it isn't the boy wonder!'

'Hello, Farrow, you old sod,' he grinned. 'D'you want to risk it, or will you walk—hey!

204

You been in a fight, or something?'

'All right, you can kiss him better later,' Charlie said. 'Did you get the car laid on?'

Sam winked at me and nodded at Charlie. 'Just like you said, Chas. Everything's set.'

'Right, then. Let's get on with it.'

We helped push Chisholm and his captor up into the cabin, and climbed in beside them. Sam hit the button, and the protesting whine of the starter motor rose to a peevish scream. The engine coughed once or twice, then caught with a roar. The blades picked up speed, and there was a little jerk as we lifted off. I put my mouth close to Charlie's ear and yelled above the racket.

'Charlie, listen. There's this feller called Petch . . .'

He put a hand on my arm and nodded and I watched his mouth form the words. He told me he knew about Petch, and that we could talk later. I could not imagine how he'd found out, but was quite content to take his word for it. Trying to talk above all that din required the sort of effort I wasn't keen to make. So I looked out of the little perspex window and watched the lifeboat station fall away behind and below us. I could still just see, way out in the mouth of the estuary, the riding lights of the timber ship. I wondered what the skipper had said when he was told what I'd done to the radio gear. One thing was certain. Unless they had a batch of pigeons on board, they were not going to be sending any messages. To Petch, or to anyone else.

We swung away south from the river and clattered on through the night sky with the lights of roads and towns spread out a thousand feet below us. I recognised Scunthorpe by the pillars of fire from its enormous chemical plant, and was able about ten minutes later to identify the big roundabout at the northern end of the Doncaster bypass. We began soon afterwards to lose height, and the engine note changed as Sam eased back on the throttle. Below us now, a disjointed stream of fast-moving vehicles sped up and down the dark M1 like so many Dinky toys on a model race track. Sam put the bird in a nose-down attitude and followed the road south. A few minutes later he found what he was looking for, and we levelled off gently as he prepared to set her down. We landed in a field alongside the motorway but just far enough away from it to avoid causing a pile-up. Charlie jumped down to the ground before the rotors stopped whirling, and helped the Siamese twins out.

'Sam, you wait here with the kite. You want to stay too, Farrow, or will you come with us?'

'I'll come with you,' I said. 'I need the exercise.' I wondered why he called Harvey 'Sam' and me 'Farrow'. I got down stiffly and followed them across the field towards the road.

We straggled over a little rise, and there it was below us. There was a car parked on the hard shoulder of the south-bound carriageway, a black Rover. As we half ran down the slope towards it, a man got out. He opened the nearside rear door and the bloke who was handcuffed to Chisholm pulled him inside. The driver made to slam the door shut, but Charlie stopped him. He leaned on the top of the sill, and ducked his head in.

'Don't forget what I told you. This is a prize specimen. Lose him and the Man will have your guts for garters!'

'Yes, mate,' I butted in, 'and I'll have your balls for a bow tie!'

'All right, Farrow.' Charlie slammed the car door shut and waved for the driver to get on his way. We watched the Rover pull out into the traffic, then lost it as he started to overtake. Charlie sighed, and we turned away to climb the slope. When we had topped it, and could see the dark shape of the helicopter across the wide field, Charlie pulled something out of his raincoat pocket and held out his hand.

'I think this is yours. You ought to be more damned careful with your stuff!'

It was my pipe. Immediately, I knew where he must have found it.

'You picked it up at Petch's place,' I said. 'Did you get my jacket, too?'

'No, just the pipe. It was wedged between

one of the beds and the wall. Petch cleared away everything else, but that he overlooked.'

'But how did you get on to him?'

'We had a lot of help,' Charlie said. 'Most of it from a sixty-year-old unemployed mill worker called John James Boardman. He walked into Brighouse police station at ten o'clock this morning'—Charlie broke off and looked at the illuminated dial of his watch—'just about twelve hours ago. He wanted to confess to the killing of little Christine Palmer. Remember little Christine Palmer?'

I said I did, and Charlie nodded. We had paused halfway across the field, and I fought the impulse to ask Charlie if it would be all right to sit down. I didn't ask him, and he went on.

'Well, Boardman was anxious and able to prove his story, so friend Simmonds was left suddenly with a lot of spare men on his hands.'

'So he put them to work doing what?' The interruption was in no way necessary. I just didn't want Charlie to think I was too tired to make my usual contribution. The fact that I *was* too tired only helped make me do it.

'Checking the Firearms Register, that's what. Then making a detailed list of every permit holder in the Huddersfield area—all bloody four hundred and seventy-eight of them.'

'So what made the tall, cool, and perfectly lovely Petch stand out from all the rest of the

208

sharpshooters?'

'Nothing—at first. At first he was just one of the forty-odd people on our list who lived within one-mile radius of the town centre. We called on every one. All but seven were members of a rifle club, and seemed on the face of it to be O.K.'

'What about the seven suspects?'

'We gave them the fine-toothcomb treatment. Petch wasn't at home, so we gave his house the treatment. We found a lovely little Brno with a telescopic sight, fired recently and not since cleaned. The marks on the cartridge cases weren't conclusive, of course. They never are. But this time they didn't need to be. I recognised that stinking pipe of yours.'

'Awfully nice of you to bring it back,' I said. He ignored that one.

'After that it was simple. We found out that Petch makes a trip to Hull every Monday and Thursday, to buy his fish straight from the dock. Sometimes he gets back in time to open up for the evening trade, sometimes he just doesn't bother.'

'Don't his customers get a bit fed up with that?'

'Not really. And that was something else. Petch's fish and chips are lousy. Why would he drive all the way across to Hull to buy his own fish, then ruin it by doing his frying in oil? Most of his customers are Pakistanis, people who don't know good fish and chips from a hole in the ground. But even *they* don't care very much whether he opens or not. So why go to all that bother?'

'The timber ships,' I said. Every time Charlie and I got to talking we seemed to wind up doing this kind of ventriloquist-and-dummy routine.

'Right,' he said. We resumed our walk across the dark field, back towards the flying machine. 'The timber ships. In and out of Hull all the time. Sailors off them are damn nearly as familiar in the pubs around the docks as deck-hands off the trawlers. Perfect, isn't it?'

'Perfect,' I agreed. 'So you found out there was a Russian ship leaving on the tide, and organised your little hovering act. Tell me, Charlie—what would you have done if I hadn't busted loose?'

'We had a Fishery Protection vessel on the way,' he said. 'The helicopter was just to watch they didn't wrap you both in a couple of fathoms of cable chain and dump you over the side.'

'They wouldn't have done that to Chisholm.'

'Wouldn't they? You never know. Anyway'— Charlie gave me a boost up into the helicopter cabin—'let's get out of here. We've got work to do yet.'

'Like what?' I said. Charlie turned his bland stare on me.

'Like Petch,' he said. 'He wasn't back before

210

I left Huddersfield. Now, he may be. Of course, I would have saved him for you, in any case. You all set?'

I said I was and Charlie gave Sam Harvey the signal to take off. This time we were in the air no longer than five or ten minutes. We landed gently with all the room in the world, right in the middle of Huddersfield Town's football pitch. We got out, crouching unnecessarily beneath the *whop-whopping* rotor blades, and waved to Harvey as he lifted the machine up and away again. He gave us a thumbs up, and was gone. We crossed the dark and deserted stadium, me shivering a little from the chill. Charlie had the Rover parked in the road outside the ground. As we moved up to it I sensed a slight movement in the deep shadow by one of the turnstiles, and caught sight of red sparks as someone dropped a cigarette end. I made a grab at my waistband. Charlie put his hand on my arm.

'Easy, Farrow. Bloody marvellous, isn't it?' Then, louder: 'That you, Constable?'

He moved up on us in his big creaking boots. He got close enough to peer into Charlie's face, and we could hear the soft mumblings from his little pocket radio. He coughed, and touched the neb of his bobby's helmet.

'S'right, sir. I 'eered the 'elicopter, an' thowt you'd be along in a minute.'

'Yes. Well, now—what's the good word from your lot?'

'Inspector ses to tell you that Petch is back, sir. He's back, but he never opened the shop. He must 'ave thowt it were too late, like.'

'Very likely. Do you want a lift into town?'

The constable said no thanks, and we got in. Charlie swung the Rover hard left into Leeds Road. I asked him if there was a duster in the car. He said no, but I would find a packet of paper hankies in the glove compartment. I got them out, and went to work on the Smith & Wesson. I ejected the fat bright shells, wiped each of them carefully, and put the spent one in my pocket. When I had done my best with the pistol I reloaded the cylinder, taking care to see that the empty chamber was last in line. Charlie nodded, his eyes on the road.

'How the hell did you manage to hang on to that thing?'

'I didn't,' I said. 'They took it away from me. But I told them as I was leaving that if they made me go home without it you'd almost certainly be angry.'

'Jock always said you were a bit of a mad bastard, Farrow. I didn't know which kind of mad he meant.'

'Do you know now?'

'No, and I don't suppose I ever will. Put the safety on, for Christ's sake! And point it the other way.'

'You just better make sure that *yours* is

working, mate. That bloody Petch is going to need a lot of persuading.'

'A tough boy, eh?'

'Tough is correct,' I said, 'and I'm not feeling exactly on top of my form. So don't let's take any chances, Charlie. All right?'

I tucked the pistol into my waistband. We had run straight through the town centre, and were driving slowly along the Manchester Road. Charlie was leaning forward over the wheel to watch for his turning. He pulled right into Whiteley Street, and drew up a few minutes later in the gloomy little forecourt of Milnsbridge railway station. He switched off, set the handbrake, and checked his pistol. We got out, and locked up.

The cobbled back streets of Milnsbridge are still lit by gas lamps, and not too many of them. I for one was glad of the friendly dark. We walked for three or four minutes, then Charlie touched my arm.

'It's this next one. Hartley Street. Petch's place is down at the other end, last on the left. Simmonds has a man on the job. We'll find him first.'

Finding him was easy. Very much too easy. We crossed the top of Hartley Street and stood in the shadow cast by the gable of the end house. The buildings were terraced, and the second one down was some kind of shop. In the darkness of the set-back doorway, a cigarette glowed. Charlie cursed.

'Get that silly born bastard over here.'

I groped around in the gutter and found a couple of little stones. When I tossed the first one, his cigarette went out. I tossed the second, and stepped out into the feeble light of the corner gas lamp, so that he could see me. I beckoned, and he hurried across. Charlie tore into him.

'Can't you buggers go five minutes without making bloody smoke signals? Why didn't you just send him a telegram, and be done with it?' He started to stammer, and Charlie cut him short. 'Never mind that now. Find a telephone and organise a Black Maria. Tell them to get here as fast as they can.'

The C.I.D. man made to move off across the top of the street. Charlie grabbed his arm and hauled him back. 'Not that way, for God's sake! He's probably seen enough of you as it is.'

He walked quickly away. We followed him as far as the next right turn, then cut off round the block to come up at the bottom end of Hartley Street, right on Petch's corner. It was still not turning-out time for the pubs and cinemas, and the streets were quiet. A taxi turned into Hartley Street and stopped about halfway up on the other side. Two couples got out, and we heard their laughter. A door slammed, and the taxi drew away. We stepped around the corner, and stood with our backs pressed against the double doors of Petch's lean-to. Light shone through the thin curtains drawn across the window of the room above the shop, but the rest of the place was in darkness. Charlie put his mouth close to my ear and began to whisper. Then we heard the van start up. Whatever plan Charlie had, he changed it in that one instant.

'We'll take him as he opens up!'

But he never did open up. We stepped apart with our guns in our fists, each with his back against one of the doors. Inside, the motor roared. I heard the clashing of gears, and yelled a warning.

'Charlie—look out!'

There was a terrific rending crash as the lock smashed, and the doors were flung wide. The one on my side caught me a buffeting swipe and hurled me to the ground. I fell heavily on my right side, but twisted over to bring up the Smith & Wesson. The grey van hurtled backwards into the street, its tyres screeching hideously as Petch hauled the wheel hard round. He had the headlights full on, and the glare was blinding. He was in a forward gear, and bearing down fast, before I could get up on my elbow for a shot. Then the blast of Charlie's .357 was dinning in my ears, and I saw the windscreen go. I shot for the tyres, triggering fast. The van slewed round at a crazy angle and crashed head-on into a house across the way. The window went in with an enormous splintering crash. The motor stalled and quite suddenly, just for an instant, there was silence. Then I was scrambling to my feet and falling back on my knees again with wood from the outhouse door flying off in splinters just above my head. The night seemed filled with the massive boom of Petch's big .45 and the sharper crack of Charlie's .357.

Petch was out of the van and away in a staggering dash down the street. As he ran, he was twisted half round to shoot back at us. I scrambled up, and Charlie ran out into the middle of the road. He stood there, stock-still beside the van, and I saw him raise both arms. A .45 slug ripped into a tyre, and there was a furious hiss of escaping air. I swung the sights on Petch for a fast snap shot, and let go. The hammer dropped on an empty shell.

'Charlie!' I screamed hoarsely, 'shoot, man! For Christ's sake, shoot!'

As though waiting for my instruction, Charlie squeezed off. Petch swung half round, and slammed against the wall. We heard the clatter as his fallen pistol hit the pavement. He seemed to hang for a second, then crumpled. When we got to him he was dead, his head hung backwards over the worn stone kerb. The empty eyes stared up at us with blank unconcern. Charlie bent over to pick up the .45 and put it in his pocket. We stood there looking down at him.

'Well, Charlie,' I said tiredly, 'this is one time when the party goes on *your* expenses.'

He looked up straight into my eyes, and it was the first time I could ever be certain that he really did smile. 'That's all right, Marcus,' he said. 'Be my guest.'

'Jesus, Charlie'—I shrugged to find words—'such familiarity. You disappoint me.'

'Don't I always?'

He grinned again, and I actually felt myself warm to him. Suddenly, everything he had ever said, ever done, was O.K. Had we been football players, I might have kissed him. As it was, the moment passed. Doors were opening, and people were venturing out into the street. A big old Black Maria swung round the corner, and disgorged policemen. Those in uniform began at once to shoo the yammering bystanders back into their homes. Next on the scene was a smart white Jaguar with a flashing blue light on the dome. Simmonds climbed out of it, and spotted us standing there over Petch's body. He came up running.

'You got him, then?'

'Oh yes, we got him.' Charlie nudged the body with the toe of his shoe. 'Simmonds—can we leave your people to clear this lot away for us? Farrow here has had a hard day. I want to get him back to his hotel.'

We left them to it, and walked slowly back to the Rover. The grinding hunger which had

ravaged me all day was gone. I was past it. All I
could feel now was an unutterable weariness.
Charlie seemed to sense it. He drove me back to
the George with not another word. I got out
stiffly. As I made to close the door, he leaned
across.

'We'll wrap it up tomorrow. All right?'

'All right,' I said.

FRIDAY

They told me, when I came down next
morning, that breakfast was finished. I asked
what the hell they meant. They said they
stopped serving at half past nine, and that it was
already a quarter past ten. I sat down in the
empty dining room and told them to get me
sausages, bacon, grilled tomatoes, and three
poached eggs. They got the manager instead.
He came up fast, prepared to make a thing
about it. I asked him which he would rather I
did, pay him his five days' money or have him
sue me for it. He picked the one I knew he
would and I said all right then, he better tell his
kitchen staff to get their fingers out. A large pot
of *fresh* tea, and the bacon well done.

I realised soon as I got up to the desk that I
had lost my credit cards, and had no money. I
checked the figures, anyway, and while I was

218

doing so the receptionist remembered that she had something for me. A sealed envelope. She watched curiously as I tore open the flap, and when I shook out the money her painted eyes opened wide. I pushed four of the lovely blue fivers across the desk, and gave her a wink.

'Take it out of that, love.'

There was a note in the envelope, and some nice new plastic credit cards just like the old ones I'd lost. The former said I should use the latter with my customary discretion. It also said to take it easy, that the writer was attending to certain matters, and what about meeting up at my favourite hostelry for an early lunch. The girl stuck a pink receipt slip on my bill, and watched me pick up the change. She said she hoped I had enjoyed my stay, and to come back soon. I said I would, hefted the suitcase with not much more in it than my shaving kit and the Smith & Wesson, and stepped outside into the refreshing drizzle.

The elderly assistant in the multiple tailor's looked at me queerly, but said nothing. He just asked me if I wanted something similar to the suit I'd bought the other day, or would I prefer a change. Oh, definitely a change, I said. Perhaps something rather better. His manner said at once that now I was talking. He brought out his good stuff, and I picked me a handsome one. I had already spent most of what was left of Charlie's cash money on shoes and socks and

219

a shirt and underwear, so emerged from the changing room almost literally a new man. The suit was a good fit, and the assistant fussed around me as though I was being sent out to represent the shop. I got him to make up a parcel of the clothes I had taken off, and borrowed his pen to print on it the address of the Spurn Head lifeboat station. He said yes, of course, and sent a boy out to post it right away. I was, after all, fast becoming a regular customer.

It was now half past eleven, and they were open. I debated whether to have one in town, or go straight out to the Three Nuns. I remembered Sadie, and the Three Nuns won. I walked down to the bus station, boarded a red single-decker with LEEDS on the front, and rode right to the door for five new pence. The nubile Sadie was there at her place behind the bar, and I got a grand quick smile.

'Hello, love. I say—what on earth have you done to your face?' Last time, of course, I'd had my sunglasses on. I put fingertips to the cut, which, in spite of the busted stitch, was beginning to heal well. The bruising, though, still looked ugly. Sadie eyed it with real concern, her lips puckered sympathetically. 'Oooohh . . . it looks *awful*!'

'Oh, it's not so bad,' I said bravely. 'Look, what about a Canadian Club, with plenty of ice. Make it a large one, love.' She served me the drink, and I gave her the last of Charlie's quids. 'And have one yourself.'

She paused with one hand on the till, and looked back over her shoulder. 'Thanks very much. Is it all right if I have a gin and tonic?'

'You,' I said, 'can have anything you like lass. Anything.'

She didn't simper, or come back with any of the usual snappy answers. She just smiled and looked right at me and I thought I detected a little nod. Mad Mark Farrow. Women everywhere. All the way from Kitzbuhel to Huddersfield. Only thing wrong, he never gets time to do anything constructive about any damn one of them.

'Well, cheers.'

'Cheers, love,' she said. Then: 'Oh look, there's your friend.'

'Give him a bitter lemon,' I said.

Charlie went straight to the table in the far corner, and I carried the drink over to him. He sniffed at it suspiciously, then took a tentative sip. He eyed the clothes, and cast a glance under the table at my shoes. I decided at once that last night had been an illusion.

'It's all right, Charlie,' I said. 'You're safe enough. I tasted it myself.'

'Really? Your guts'—he nodded significantly at my whisky—'must have wondered what the hell hit them. Anyway, cheers.'

It was not much more than two hours since

I'd put away the huge breakfast, but I was hungry again. I ate a good lunch. Charlie had a cheese omelette and a glass of water, and told me about his busy morning. We went very carefully over everything I could remember since Chisholm slugged me in the cinema car park, and Charlie said he reckoned we had cleaned the Huddersfield cell right out. I asked him what now. He said he was going down to make a personal report to the Man and that, if I wanted to, I could come with him. We were moving back to the saloon to have our coffee there.

'Only if I want to?'

'Yes. If you like, you can just go straight home.'

'How?'

'What d'you mean—"how"?'

'I mean how the hell am I supposed to get there?'

'Well ... I don't know. There's a train across, isn't there?'

'A train?' I said. 'Not bloody likely! What? After Rovers and helicopters and bloody private aeroplanes? The hell with that for a lark. No, Charlie ... here ...' I gave him my bundle of receipts. 'There's your chits. Give me some more cash, and I'll get a mini-cab.'

'More cash! Good God almighty, Farrow —what do you do with it all?' He tucked the bills I gave him safely away into a compartment of his wallet, and took out four more fivers. I picked them up, and stuffed them with deliberate nonchalance into the breast pocket of my jacket. He nodded. 'That's right. Easy come ... I'm beginning to wonder if the Section can afford you, matey. You must get through more money than the Man himself.'

'Yes,' I said. 'Well, you see, Charlie, it's the silver-spoon syndrome. Didn't *your* mother put one in *your* mouth?'

'We never had a mother. We were too poor.'

He stood up, and left me sitting there with my mouth open. His glasses seemed to twinkle, and I started to like him all over again. I mean, what the hell can one *do* with a guy like that. Before I could think of something, he was his old self.

'Well, I'm off.' He looked at his watch. 'Nearly half past one. I should be down there just before five. You'd better leave me a number.'

'A number?'

'Yes you know, a number,' he said sarcastically. 'In case the Man wants to ring you up and ask what you did with all the money.'

I looked over towards the bar and caught Sadie watching us with a sort of wistful expression on her face. Our eyes met and she smiled. I got up.

'Charlie,' I said, 'hang on just a minute, will you?'

I went across to the bar and asked for a small brandy. She gave me what looked like a large one and charged me for a small one. But I had made up my mind, anyway. It was still two and a half days to the end of my spring week, so why not. As she was giving me my change, I covered one of her hands. She just let it lay there, cool and smooth.

'You got any rooms here, Sadie?'

'Yes ... I mean, no ... I mean we do, but I think we're full. But I'll ask for you, if you like. How long would it be for?'

I left my hand where it was, and so did she. 'Oh, just for one night—on this occasion, that is. I thought I'd stay over and have a bit of a break. I like the company.'

She pulled her hand gently away and looked down at the bar to count my change just one more time. The back of her neck, with its little tendrils of soft hair, turned a dull red.

'Well, if it's only for one night you could—I mean, if we're full up here ... I've got a spare room at my place ...' She looked at me then, and her voice quickened. 'It's not much, but you'd be welcome. I don't usually ... I mean, I wouldn't want you to think ...'

'Sadie, love,' I said, 'bless you.' Her face now was crimson. 'I wouldn't even begin to think anything of the sort. Listen—this isn't your night off, by any chance?'

'I could take it off.'

'Right, then,' I said. 'That's settled. Oh, one more thing. Are you on the phone at home?'

She said she was, and gave me the number. I went back and told it to Charlie. He was standing at the door, waiting to be off. He gave me his blank stare, then shot a glance at Sadie, busy now with a couple of customers.

'What was all that about?'

'Look, Charlie,' I said, 'I'm on holiday—remember? You mind your business, and I'll mind mine.'

He opened the door, and turned to go. 'Sure,' he said, 'if that's the way you want it. I just hope she's not too disappointed, that's all. You're no young buck, Farrow, and you've had a trying week. We wouldn't want you to overtax yourself.'

I opened my mouth to tell him to bollocks, but he was through the door and away. I stepped to the window and watched him get into the Rover. He pulled out of the car park, swung round the roundabout, and shot off on the Mirfield Road towards the M1. He never once looked back.

Photoset, printed and bound in Great Britain by
REDWOOD PRESS LIMITED, Melksham, Wiltshire